# "What are you doing?" Sarah gasped

All her muscles tightened at Brett's touch. "What's the matter?"

"Nothing's the matter. But I never could resist a challenge. And you're certainly a challenge, Sarah Malone." His thumb began to stroke her skin very slowly, just below her earlobe, sending shafts of shivering anticipation down her spine.

"Don't," she whispered. "Brett, please . . ."

"Why not? What are you afraid of, Sarah. I promise I won't bite. At least not without an invitation."

Now his thumb was moving in feather-light circles, tracing the base of her throat. Sarah closed her eyes, and she felt his warm breath against her cheek.

"Is that an invitation?" he asked softly.

Sarah opened her mouth to say no, but it was too late. . . .

**Kay Gregory** grew up in England, but moved to Canada as a teenager. She now lives in Vancouver with her husband, two sons, one dog and two ferrets. She has had innumerable jobs, some interesting, some extremely boring, which have often provided background for her books. Now that she is writing Harlequin romance novels, Kay thinks she has at last found a job that she won't find necessary to change.

## Books by Kay Gregory

### HARLEQUIN ROMANCE

2919—A STAR FOR A RING
3016—A PERFECT BEAST
3058—IMPULSIVE BUTTERFLY
3082—AMBER AND AMETHYST
3152—YESTERDAY'S WEDDING

### HARLEQUIN PRESENTS

1352—THE MUSIC OF LOVE

# BREAKING THE ICE
## Kay Gregory

*Harlequin Books*

TORONTO • NEW YORK • LONDON
AMSTERDAM • PARIS • SYDNEY • HAMBURG
STOCKHOLM • ATHENS • TOKYO • MILAN
MADRID • WARSAW • BUDAPEST • AUCKLAND

To Jo & Jim Slade, without whose help I would
never have found the time to write my books, and
to their daughter, Heather.

Original hardcover edition published in 1991
by Mills & Boon Limited

ISBN 0-373-03206-4

Harlequin Romance first edition July 1992

BREAKING THE ICE

# CHAPTER ONE

IT WAS the feet Sarah noticed first. Big ones, in mud-caked brown hiking boots. And they were sticking out from under her new couch almost as if they belonged there. She closed her eyes, and then opened them again quickly. The feet were still there.

And of course they didn't belong in her living room at all.

She took a step closer and realized that it wasn't just a matter of feet. Brown woolen socks covered solid ankles, and long legs extended up to firm, corduroy-clad thighs. One of the legs was bent slightly at the knee, but the other stretched out endlessly across her carpet. As Sarah's eyes traveled disbelievingly upward, she saw that the corduroy covered more than just legs and thighs. This vision protruding from beneath her couch was visible as far as the waist, and the view exposed by the hip-hugging beige trousers was altogether attractive. Yes. She swallowed. Very attractive indeed.

She pushed at the short wisps of brown hair which fanned out over her ears and took a long, very deep breath. Was she going crazy? There appeared to be a dead body on her floor, and she was standing here mesmerized, admiring it as if she were some silly moon-struck adolescent—possibly with necrophiliac leanings.

Without releasing her breath, she extended a tentative hand and placed it lightly on the back of the nearest ankle. Immediately it moved, and a man's deep voice growled threateningly, "Hairy little horror. Just wait till I get my hands on you, Houdini. This is the last time

I'm going through this, my friend, and you had better believe it.''

Sarah jumped backward. Oh, Lord! That wasn't any dead body lying at her feet, as she ought to have known from the beginning.

She had a real live hunk on her hands—or the bottom half of one, at least.

She took a firm grip on the back of the nearest chair as a demonstrably living body eased itself out from under the pale gray fabric. "I do believe it," she said fervently. "And as this is my house, and that's my floor you're making so free with, it most certainly *will* be the last time you go through this, whoever you are." She watched, fascinated, as the rest of the intruder emerged into the soft September dusk, and added faintly, "And as I'm not particularly hairy, I sincerely hope this is a case of mistaken identity. I've no intention of letting you get your hands on me, Mr.——"

She stopped abruptly.

The top half of the figure rising slowly to its feet was just as appealing as the bottom, and for one mad, illogical moment Sarah thought she wouldn't at all mind him getting his big hands on certain parts of her. He was tall, big, with a strong, very masculine face under wildly disheveled reddish brown hair, and as Sarah stood stunned, gaping at him, he took a step toward her.

She saw something flare in the dark-lashed tawny gold eyes as they traveled smoothly over her which looked remarkably like admiration—and that surprised her almost as much as it irritated her, because her sensible brown tweed suit had been chosen specifically for its discouraging severity.

A smile spread across the man's face, a wide, full-lipped smile that was as attractive as the rest of him, and it did strange things to Sarah's stomach as he answered softly, "That's too bad."

She stared at him suspiciously. "What is?"

"That you've no intention of letting me get my hands on——"

He got no further. Sarah's face flamed with furious color as she interrupted bitingly, "Mr. . . . Whoever You Are, as I said before, this is *my* house, and I'll thank you to get out of it. Right now."

"Jackson," he replied, as if he hadn't even heard her. "Brett Jackson. And I apologize for the intrusion, Mrs. . . .?"

"Miss Malone," said Sarah through gritted teeth. "Goodbye, Mr. Jackson." Ridiculously, she held out her hand.

And, even more ridiculously, he took it.

"Miss Malone, I really do apologize." He *sounded* sincere, and the planes of his face were smoothed into serious lines. If there had not been an ill-concealed hint of laughter in his eyes, she might have been totally taken in.

Sarah pulled her hand away and said briskly, "Apology accepted. Goodbye, Mr. Jackson—again."

"Don't you even want an explanation?"

"Not particularly." She did, but she wasn't going to admit it. This man was altogether too unnerving and she would feel safer with him well out of her way. Other than her father and the plumber, she hadn't had a man in her house for years, let alone an uninvited stranger— who in spite of his engaging smile had an aura of dangerous sensuality about him.

He was leaning against the wall now with his ankles crossed and his arms folded loosely on his chest. "Well, whether you want it or not, Miss Malone," he informed her, "as we're going to be neighbors from now on, I owe you an explanation. So you're going to get it."

"Neighbors?" croaked Sarah.

He nodded. "That's what I said. I've just bought the house next door."

"You—you mean the old Francelli house? But that's been sold to some man with a kid who runs an animal clinic in Port Angeles."

"Guilty as charged." The irritating intruder bowed from the waist, smiling complacently.

"Oh, but I thought..." What had she thought? Not much, really, except that if the new owner worked miles away in Port Angeles she wouldn't see much of him. The small community on the north coast of the Olympic Peninsula where she had lived and worked all her life was used to people who occupied their houses almost exclusively during the summer, and for some reason she had thought he'd be one of those.

"I thought you weren't moving in yet," she finished lamely.

He shrugged. "Sorry to disappoint you but, as you see, you were misinformed."

"Yes, I do see. What have you done with your son, then?"

"Ah, yes. You mentioned you'd heard about Tony." He cocked an eyebrow at the sort of angle not normally achieved except between the pages of a book.

"Not much happens in a place like this," she explained ruefully. "The grapevine works exceptionally fast."

"I suppose so. Tony's at school, if it matters to you. He started today."

"Yes, of course." Sarah was beginning to relax. "What were you doing under my couch, Mr. Jackson?" She had to know.

"My name's Brett. We're going to be neighbors, after all. Do you have a name besides Malone?"

"It's Sarah." Why did she feel that aggravating tightness in her chest?

"That's a pretty, old-fashioned sort of name. Like its owner?" He raised an eyebrow again, this time in taunting inquiry.

"No, not at all like its owner," snapped Sarah. "Mr. Jackson—Brett—what were you doing in my house?"

"He sighed. "Looking for Fawcett."

"For what?"

"Fawcett. He's my son's ferret. A big, stupid albino with a passion for running away. He's the reason I bought the house in such a hurry. When my wife died, Tony and I moved to an apartment. We'd been there almost three years when Tony got Fawcett. The third time he escaped and turned up in our landlady's bread box, she kicked us out. She doesn't like ferrets." He held out his palms and tried, unsuccessfully, to look bewildered.

"I wonder why not," murmured Sarah dryly.

"Can't think. Anyway, it was time we got a place in the country. More space. And Tony wants a dog."

"I see," replied Sarah, as visions of endless raids on her property to retrieve lost animals ran uneasily through her head.

"Yes, so if you——" Brett broke off with startling abruptness as something fast and white darted across the floor, nattering softly, and disappeared behind a chair.

"Aha! Got you." He lunged across the floor, pushing Sarah summarily out of the way, dived over her coffee table and, with a shout of triumph, stood up clutching what looked like a white fur muff with teeth.

Against the wall, Sarah's plain but expensive teak lamp stand teetered and almost fell.

"I think," she said frigidly, "that it's time you left—Brett."

He nodded, holding the squirming little animal by the scruff of its neck and glaring at it. "Yes. I think you're right." He loped across the room with an easy, devastatingly virile gait, and when he reached the door he turned and added severely, "By the way, if you don't want strangers under your furniture looking for ferrets, you should be more careful about locking your doors. The wind must have blown it open."

Sarah scowled at him. "And you should be more careful where you put your feet. There's mud all over my carpet."

He glanced down. "Good grief, so there is. I apologize—again. I'm afraid I stopped off earlier to see a man with a couple of pigs."

Pigs, thought Sarah. It figures. But aloud she only said, "Never mind. It won't be hard to clean up."

Brett flashed her another stomach-churning, not very repentant grin before he disappeared down the steps.

She stared at the door which he had closed very deliberately behind him—and which she almost always did keep locked. But she had been in a hurry this morning, having slept in after one of her frequent restless nights, and although Angela Baddeley, who was the town's lawyer as well as Sarah's friend and employer, would not have minded much, Sarah hated being late.

Slowly she crossed the room and sank down into the square, not very comfortable chair which matched the couch.

She shook her head. What an extraordinary encounter. It was years since a man had looked at her in that sexy, speculative way. And—she had to admit it—that was probably because she'd discouraged speculation. There had been several men in the beginning after

Jason—she'd gone out with a few of them—and they had certainly tried to get through the wall she had erected so painstakingly around her emotions. Nice men, most of them, but after a few dates they had given up, iced out by her lack of response. And she hadn't cared because at first she'd been hurting too much to endure even the thought of intimacy. After a while, when the wound began to heal, as most nonfatal wounds did, she had felt safer, less vulnerable, behind her frozen barricade. With it safely in place, no one could break her heart again. She knew people sometimes called her "the ice-maiden," but that had long since ceased to worry her. It was true that she was often chilled and solitary behind her protective shield, as if she were indeed sculpted out of ice. But it was comfortable enough. Safe—and she had no particular wish to see it pierced.

Frowning, and wondering why she felt more restless and dissatisfied than she had in months, she jumped to her feet and slammed a frying pan on to the stove with entirely unnecessary force.

Sarah stirred and moved her head on the pillow. Vaguely she was conscious of warmth stealing through the curtains which she rarely bothered to close, and she thought how pleasant it was to lie in bed knowing she would get up to the cheerful comfort of an unseasonably warm September. That dream she'd just had—it had been pleasant too. Something about a white, fast, furry animal and a man who was not Jason...

She stretched lazily, smiling with contented indolence—and then, in an instant, the smile was wiped from her face as the morning quiet was shattered by a noise which to Sarah's ears sounded like an assault force going over the top in her garden.

She wrestled the sheets away and struggled to a sitting position. What was happening? Was she being invaded, and if so, by whom? Still groggy with sleep, she staggered over to the window. And it was no invading army which met her accusing eye but her new neighbor's glisteningly naked torso. His long, muscled arms were raised above his head and he was wielding a purposeful hammer as he rained blows down at something on the other side of the fence. To make matters worse, he was making a sound which she supposed was meant to be singing.

She blinked, and smoothed a hand over her tousled hair. What was this naked man doing at—she glanced at her watch—eight o'clock on a Saturday morning, attacking some unseen and unfortunate object with enthusiasm and noise enough to wake the dead? Well, maybe not the dead, she amended, but certainly Sarah Malone. And why wasn't he wearing any clothes? Not that the view was unimpressive...

And that's enough of that, my girl, she told herself firmly as the last vestiges of sleep vanished and she came fully and furiously awake. The man wasn't naked, he just had his shirt off, and the inconsiderate jerk hadn't given a damn that his only neighbor might still be fast asleep.

There was a momentary pause in the hammering as Brett ran a handkerchief across his gleaming brow. He was just raising his arm to strike again when Sarah flung open the window.

"What on earth do you think you're doing, Brett Jackson?" she shouted. "Don't you know it's only eight o'clock?"

Startled, Brett lowered the hammer and rested his forearms on the fence.

"Did I wake you?" He sounded surprised.

"What do you think?" asked Sarah sarcastically.

"Mmm. I guess I did. Sorry. I'm so used to getting up for Tony and animals that I sometimes forget other people like to sleep in. I'm building a kennel for the dog," he explained, as if that excused everything. He passed the now saturated handkerchief around the back of his neck. "Anyway, seeing that you're well and truly awake, I might as well carry on with the job."

He started to turn away, and Sarah, glaring at his deeply tanned back, felt resentment well up in her like a tide. How dared this arrogant, casually inconsiderate man just shrug off the fact that he'd disturbed her and carry calmly on with his morning-shattering work?

"I suppose," she shouted down at him, "that it doesn't matter to you one bit that you've ruined my Saturday's rest."

He turned back. "I'm not going to lose any sleep over it," he admitted, picking the one phrase calculated to inflame her further. "But if you want the truth—yes, it does bother me. I can't do anything to change it, that's all."

"You can shut up long enough to let me eat my breakfast in peace," retorted Sarah, determined that, if her plans for the morning were to be derailed so thoughtlessly, then so were his.

Brett's arms returned to the fence. "Breakfast?" he queried, with unmistakable hope. "I suppose I could take a few minutes off..."

"Good," said Sarah, not responding to this blatant appeal to her hospitable instincts. "Then do it."

Brett threw back his head and for the first time that morning really looked at her. When his lips began to curve up in a tantalizing smile, Sarah had a sudden, uncomfortable feeling that something was radically wrong.

She glanced down and, to her horror, saw immediately what was providing him with so much free entertainment. He might be naked to the waist, but she was almost as exposed herself through the soft nylon folds of her nightgown which, she suspected, left nothing to the imagination. Not that Brett Jackson appeared to suffer from lack of imagination. Quite the opposite.

Cheeks reddening, Sarah reached for the curtains and called irritably, "Oh, finish your kennel if you like. What difference does it make now?"

But as she pulled the ice-blue curtains firmly across the window she was sure she heard the sound of a man's deep laugh, pealing out full-throated and vibrant on the morning air.

"Self-satisfied jerk," she muttered angrily. "Inconsiderate brute." And then, unbidden and unwanted, a picture came into her mind of Brett's body shining with moisture in the early morning sun.

Deliberately she forced herself to think about breakfast instead, but as she cracked eggs into a pan she found herself remembering with a regretful, almost wistful surprise that she kind of liked a man who could use his hands...

Oh, no, you don't. You don't like anything about that man, she told herself firmly. And that glorious, supple body doesn't count.

Which made it all the more aggravating that the first thing that came into her mind that evening as she leaned over her front gate and watched her parents' car pull up was that perhaps they might have heard more about her new neighbor's past history and background than she had. Clara Malone had a talent for ferreting out information.

Ferreting... Oh, God. Why did everything lead back to that man and his dubious ménage?

"What's the matter, dear? You look—flustered." Clara's sharp, deceptively gentle eyes took in the fact that her daughter was exuding a most unusual aura of excitement. Unusual, because it was years since Sarah had permitted herself to be anything other than cool, reserved and undemonstrative. Ten years, to be accurate, thought Clara, and then she had been only seventeen.

"Nothing." Sarah pulled open the gate and ushered her parents up a neatly graveled path to the dark oak front door of her bungalow. "Nothing's the matter. It's warm for September, isn't it?"

Clara Malone recognized an evasion when she heard it. "It's been warm all summer. What's wrong, Sarah?"

"Noth—oh, all right. My day started badly, that's all. I think my new neighbor's going to be a problem."

"Brett Jackson? Oh, dear. Yes, I did hear some odd rumors about the man, but I hoped they were only gossip."

Sarah closed her eyes briefly. She knew it! Her mother had already learned his name, and no doubt by now she had also discovered his age, occupation, hobbies, club memberships and income—not to mention an accurate inventory of women friends past and present.

She took Clara's jacket and waved her to the pale gray couch. George Malone sat down beside her shaking his white head. Sarah caught his eye and tried desperately not to smile. Clara's "information network," as she and her father called it, had always been an unfailing source of amusement to them both.

Clara, who never missed anything, noted the exchange and said huffily, "If you're going to laugh at me, you two, I'm not going to tell you what I've found out."

"I may survive," murmured George dryly.

But Sarah, whose curiosity was now thoroughly aroused, was sure she wouldn't.

"We're not laughing at you," she said quickly, "and as I live next door to him, of course I'd like to know what you've heard."

"Oh, Lord," groaned George, rolling his eyes up. "I do believe it's catching. You're turning into your mother's daughter, Sarah. That's as splendidly plausible an excuse as I ever heard for nosing into someone else's business."

"There's no need to be rude, George," snapped Clara.

"It's not an excuse," Sarah mumbled, knowing perfectly well it was.

George picked up a copy of the paper from a magazine rack and started to read it for the second time that day.

"Your father has decided to ignore us," said Clara, eyeing him balefully.

"Yes," agreed Sarah. She waited a moment and then said with a sheepish smile, "Supper should be ready in a minute. What sort of rumors, Mother?" She didn't sit down, but stood hovering in the hall doorway.

Clara patted her bobbed gray head and cleared her throat importantly. "Well, he's a widower, of course."

"Yes, he told me. So did Angela, actually. She heard it from the real estate man."

"Good grief," muttered George. "If I were a fugitive from justice, I sure wouldn't try to hide out in Caley Cove."

"Well, you're not," replied his wife dampingly. She turned back to Sarah. "As a matter of fact, dear, I understand that his wife died in rather—questionable—circumstances. Leaving him with a little boy."

"Yes, he's called Tony. What circumstances?"

Clara lowered her voice. "It seems, if the rumors are true, that she killed herself. Took an overdose of sleeping pills, poor thing. But they say he drove her to it.''

"Are you sure? And who are 'they'?''

"Your mother's sources," interrupted George. "Molly Bracken at the post office, Harry Koniski at the real estate office, Doris Whatshername at the telephone exchange——"

"George, that's quite enough. It's not my fault that people talk to me." Clara sniffed.

"They talked to the Inquisition too."

"I think supper's ready. Why don't you both sit down?" suggested Sarah quickly. Her parents, who were in fact devoted to one another, had carried on in this vein for as long as she could remember. But tonight she hoped they would avoid one of their frequent rows because—she had to admit it—for once her mother had information she was surprisingly anxious, as well as a little afraid, to hear.

She waited until they were seated uneasily around her chrome and glass oval table in front of plates heaped with beef, two vegetables and crispy roast potatoes, before returning, hesitantly, to the subject of her next-door neighbor.

"How is Brett supposed to have driven his wife to suicide?" she asked, her eyes fixed firmly on a green bean.

George rolled his eyes again, but Clara ignored him and replied in an unnecessarily conspiratorial whisper, "Apparently he was having an affair with his receptionist at the animal clinic. His wife couldn't live with it. So she didn't."

"Dear heaven!" Sarah swallowed uneasily, thinking of the confident, smiling, provocative man next door. "Are you sure?"

"Well, not *sure* exactly, but Molly heard it from a very reliable source..."

George snorted, and Clara, looking defensive, gave him a dirty look and snapped her mouth shut.

Dear heaven, thought Sarah again. Suicide. No, her mother must be mistaken. It was only more Caley Cove gossip. Surely it was. Brett just didn't seem like the type who would drive a woman to take her life. Still—he *was* incredibly attractive, and that air of easy sensuality must act like a magnet to the more susceptible members of her sex. She swallowed again. How lucky she wasn't susceptible—and hadn't been for the past ten years. Oh, yes, she had learned a valuable lesson from Jason. From the sound of things, he and Brett Jackson could have a lot in common.

Funny, her food didn't seem to have much taste now, and she didn't want to talk about him any more.

But her mother did. "Why did you say he might be a problem?" Clara asked sharply, recalling her daughter's earlier comment.

"Oh, no special reason. He just makes a lot of noise in the mornings. At least he did today."

Clara wasn't satisfied, but Sarah refused to be more explicit and in the end her mother had to admit defeat.

They discussed the view from the window after that—for the hundredth time—and Sarah reiterated, also for the hundredth time, that she was delighted with her small bungalow above the cliffs overlooking the Strait of Juan de Fuca. On a soft late summer evening like today's, with the pink reflections of dusk just beginning to tint a barely ruffled sea, she could feel at peace, contented, as she sometimes wasn't within the more confined boundaries of the town.

"Yes, dear." Clara returned unerringly to the subject she wanted to discuss. "But it's so isolated. Only you and that mysterious neighbor."

"Plus the Mackenzies at the end of the road. Besides, he's hardly mysterious."

"Perhaps not, but I felt much easier about you when the Francellis lived next door."

Sarah didn't doubt that. Mrs. Francelli had reported her every move to her mother, and she had been more than relieved when the elderly couple had at last decided to move closer to the shops and services of Port Angeles.

"I'm all right, Mother," she said again. "I've lived here for the past six years, and I haven't come to the slightest harm yet."

"I know you haven't. Not yet. But you didn't have to move the moment you had enough money saved to buy a house. You could have stayed with us, dear. We were happy to have you." Clara was repeating an old grievance.

"Of course you were, and I'm grateful," replied Sarah, trying not to scream at this rehashing of a matter which had been decisively settled six years earlier although it had never for a moment been laid to rest.

Clara's eyes darted round the room, seeking another outlet for her frustration. "Your new furniture is too spartan," she complained. "All white and gray and— cold, dear. Just like your old suite. And those odd ship models on the walls. Not at all the sort of home to welcome a man."

"As I don't welcome men, that doesn't matter, does it?" said Sarah, her full, soft lips compressed.

"And that's another thing. I know your experience with Jason was unfortunate, but..."

Sarah gave up and let her mother grumble on. Her weekly dinners with her parents, either here or at their house in town, invariably degenerated into a diatribe from Clara about her daughter's home, furnishings, clothes and life-style—with emphasis on the desirability of husbands. Sarah thought she could do without one of those permanent sparring partners. Her parents might thrive on squabbles, but she didn't.

When Clara finally wound down, the three of them played Scrabble, as they did every week, and when the night was still young Clara and George went home.

Sarah worked for a short time on one of the model ships her mother had objected to, and eventually made her way along the hallway to bed.

The following morning she was again awakened early. As she struggled resentfully out of a deep sleep, once more the sound of loud and unnecessary noise came clamoring from behind the fence next door. But this time Sarah knew it was no invading army that was disturbing her slumbers. The racket drifting through her partly opened window was very obviously that of over-excited dog.

She listened carefully. Correction. Dogs. And kid. The human kind. Sighing, she looked at the clock. Nine a.m. today. She supposed she ought to be thankful for small mercies.

Muttering under her breath, she flung off the covers, wrapped a thick terry robe around her tall, slim figure, and marched across to the window.

# CHAPTER TWO

SARAH pushed the curtain indignantly aside—and immediately her eyes fell on Brett, in all his half-naked morning glory. He was bending down in a futile attempt to soothe two leaping bundles of fur. As she watched, he put a finger to his lips and glanced up at her window, apparently also trying to quieten, a small, fair-haired boy with freckles, who was jumping up and down beside him and beaming from ear to ear.

Gradually the barking and yelling tapered off, and as they did so Brett's unusual golden eyes encountered her brown ones. With an exasperated sigh she pulled viciously at the curtains, shutting out the beginnings of his curling, attractive smile.

Damn him, she thought helplessly. Damn him. Obviously with that man as a neighbor there wasn't a hope that she would ever get a weekend's rest again. And she wanted to shout at him, read him the riot act—but every time she was about to do it he turned on that sexy, impossible grin. And every time he did that her knees went mushy on her and her stomach started folding up inside.

She sighed heavily, glancing at her single bed with its woven pale blue bedspread—and quite unexpectedly a memory popped into her head of another morning, long ago, when she had woken up in a bed that was not single, and beside her there had been a man who, in some ways, was very like Brett. Although that other man had been dark and intense, where Brett was copper-haired and mocking...

She went into the bathroom and began to scrub furiously at her teeth. Why was she thinking about that faroff morning now? It was over. She was glad it was over. And she certainly wasn't interested in any further romantic involvements. Ever. Particularly not with a man who had a child, an escape artist ferret, two unruly dogs and an unholy passion for noise.

Nor did it take much brainpower to figure out that the only way to survive with Brett as a next-door neighbor was to pretend he didn't exist.

She wondered why this eminently sensible conclusion left her feeling miserably flat and dull.

On Monday evening, as Sarah pulled into her driveway after work, the first thing she heard as she switched off the engine of her Volkswagen was the sound of two animals barking an excited chorus. She looked up, and saw that the fence which divided her property from Brett's was shaking ominously. And as the barking grew louder, and she continued to stare doubtfully at the fence which looked ready to collapse beneath the onslaught, two shiny black paws appeared briefly, scrabbled, and vanished again. They were followed by two shaggy gray ones, which also disappeared after an unsuccessful attempt to scale the defenses.

Sarah watched as the black paws scrabbled once more, then, shaking her head, she walked quickly over to Brett's gate, opened it a crack, slithered through and snapped it shut behind her. Just in time. A second later she was knocked flat by two joyfully welcoming dogs who proceeded to smother her face and hands with damp kisses.

When Brett pulled up a minute or two afterward, at first he was so busy making sure that Tony cleared the station-wagon of its day's accumulation of chewing-gum wrappers, crayons, odd-shaped stones and something green and sticky of doubtful origin that he didn't notice

the commotion on his lawn. Then his eye was caught by
a flash of pale pink which he quickly realized was a wildly
kicking, nylon-covered, altogether shapely leg—ending
in a deplorably sensible brown pump. At the same
moment as he took in that the leg was attached to a body
which gave promise of being equally shapely, he heard
a woman's laugh followed by a voice shouting, "Off,
you two! Move it! I love you too, but really this is carrying things too far."

Of course. He should have recognized the trespasser
the moment he saw that plain, frantically kicking brown
shoe.

Brushing his hand over his mouth, he strolled across
toward the squirming trio.

There was a momentary lull in the activity as the dogs
paused to cock their heads at their new master, and in
the space between their ecstatically wriggling bodies
Sarah looked up to see Brett standing over her with his
hands resting carelessly on his hips. And even from this
unusual and undignified angle she was conscious of the
power of his casual and overwhelming masculinity.

As she tried to struggle to her feet, Brett leaned toward
her, but instead of attempting to help her up he grinned
broadly and asked with a mocking leer, "What's this,
Sarah Malone? Have you decided to be neighborly after
all? I must say, I could easily get used to the view." His
eyes raked appreciatively over her sprawling body and
she was sure that his practiced imagination was filling
in any details that were not immediately apparent.

At that moment the dogs returned to the attack and
another slim leg waved helplessly in the air, exposing a
tempting glimpse of pink thigh beneath the tailored tweed
skirt. "Can I join you?" he asked hopefully. "Or is this
a private party?"

Sarah choked as a wet tongue slurped her enthusiastically across the nose. "No!" she gasped, struggling desperately to push her furry tormentors away. "No, you most certainly can not join us. Please get these monsters off me."

But Brett only stood there, grinning hugely and obviously enjoying her predicament, and in the end it was Tony who distracted the dogs' attention by turning exuberant somersaults on the lawn.

"Thanks, Tony," she called breathlessly, as Brett finally rose to the occasion and took her hands to pull her to her feet. To add to her confusion, he held on to her for several deliberate seconds longer than he had to.

"How do you know I'm Tony?" shouted the owner of that name as he bounded across the grass with two delighted dogs in hot pursuit.

"Just a lucky guess," she shouted back.

Brett was looking at her with that amused, appraising expression she'd seen before, and she turned away because she was afraid that once again she was going to blush. She, who hadn't blushed for years—until he arrived on the scene.

"What was that all about, Sarah?" he asked softly, and her name whispered off his lips like a caress.

She stared at a clump of turf uprooted by the over-enthusiastic animals. "Your dogs were so pleased to see me I thought they were going to overpower the fence," she muttered. "I came over to calm them down."

"No doubt your intentions were admirable," he observed dryly. "On the other hand, I don't quite see the connection between calming them down and inciting what appeared to be a public disturbance on my lawn." He kicked reflectively at the uprooted turf on what had once been a neat patch of green.

"That wasn't my intention," she replied haughtily. "I was trying to help. Besides, it wasn't public until you two arrived."

"I might point out that this is my garden," he remarked mildly.

"Oh, well, if that's the way you feel..." She began to dust grass off her skirt.

"It's not."

As her palms brushed firmly over her thighs, Brett stretched out a hand and for a moment she was sure he was about to offer assistance. She stepped back hastily.

"It's not," he repeated. "In fact I suppose I ought to be grateful for your concern. And I'm certainly sorry if my dogs upset you."

"They didn't. Well—literally I guess they did." She smiled wryly. "But it's all right. I like dogs." She watched as the two joyful bundles of fur—one black and glossy, almost Labrador, and one gray and white, feather-tailed, almost Old English sheepdog—tumbled around the lawn after Tony.

"Do you? I thought you didn't."

"What made you think that?"

"Well, you don't have one of your own. And the expression on your charming face yesterday morning was not one of unrestrained delight."

"I don't have a dog of my own because I work all day. And as for yesterday——" She noted a slight quiver at the corner of his mouth, and explained defiantly, "As for yesterday, I'm just not very good at mornings. I'm not a nice person until I've had at least three cups of coffee."

"I don't believe it. I'm sure you're wonderful at mornings. And *very* nice."

His voice drawled lazily over the provocative words and she was sure she was not imagining the seductive gleam in his eye. Deciding this conversation was getting altogether too close to the mark, Sarah tossed her head and started to walk away.

"Sarah," he called after her, and the warmth of his tone made her hesitate. "Sarah—thanks."

As she turned to look at him he held out his hand and added with a beguiling and exaggeratedly plaintive smile, "I wish I could offer you a meal or a drink or something. But I'm afraid as we've just moved in I haven't got around to stocking up on provisions. Will you take a raincheck on it?"

"Sure." She eyed him doubtfully, wondering if he was trying to charm her into offering him dinner. If he was, the question of the moment was: did she intend to be charmed?

His hand dropped against his thigh, drawing her attention to a very appealing part of him. When she raised her eyes again hastily, she saw that he was still smiling that maddening smile. His eyes were incredibly hypnotic too—and she wasn't altogether sure she believed her mother's rumors...

"Are you trying to charm me into offering you a meal?" she demanded, surprising herself by taking the bull by the horns.

He laughed without a trace of embarrassment. "Only if I can get away with it," he admitted. "I'm a lousy cook, but I promise if you'll have us tonight I'll try to pay you back when I get some groceries in."

"Pay me back? That sounds ominous."

He shrugged, and his full lips parted in a rueful grin. "Well, you know what I mean..."

Sarah did. He wanted her to feed him—and his son—and, if she was unlucky, tomorrow or some other day he would offer to feed her in return. And she'd accept, and end up eating overcooked frozen chicken, dried-out chips and a salad which had seen better days. She sighed inwardly and decided she could cross that bridge when she came to it. At the moment it was only neighborly to have him over. Besides, he did have fascinating eyes...

"Done," she said briskly, as if they had just concluded a satisfactory business arrangement. "I'll see you and Tony in a hour. If you can wait that long."

"And if I can't?"

"Too bad. I'll still see you in an hour."

Half an hour later, after taking a casserole from the freezer and putting it in the oven, Sarah stood in front of her wardrobe studying its severely practical contents. Obviously she couldn't entertain Brett in one of her tailored suits. At least, she could, but she wouldn't feel comfortable. Then, just for a moment, to her own startled disapproval, she found herself wondering what his dead wife might have worn. A clinging, slinky skirt, perhaps? She squashed the thought disgustedly, and began to rifle busily through her clothes. Trousers were a possibility, of course, but she was well aware that all her trousers fitted her rather nicely and were the only garments she possessed which might conceivably be considered enticing. So they wouldn't do either. That left one of her three summer dresses or her neat white pleated skirt. Not the white skirt. Not with a child coming. The navy blue dress with white stripes, then? That was the one which covered her up most completely. The other two both had lower-cut necks.

She pulled on the navy blue, not bothering to look in the mirror. She knew what she'd see. A tall, almost too slim figure draped in concealing folds of navy-striped cloth. And a long neck topped by a round, pixieish face with a pointed chin and enormous dark brown eyes. Then there was her hair, short, wispy and brown, curling up obstinately around her ears. The perfect face and figure for a model, her mother had told her crossly when she'd announced she wanted to be an ordinary, unglamorous secretary to the town's lawyer instead of going on to fame and fortune in *Vogue*. But of course at that time Clara Malone hadn't absorbed the full extent of her daughter's infatuation with that lawyer. By the time the light dawned it had already been too late, and Sarah had been talking of marriage.

Now she dabbed a quick dash of powder on her nose, reapplied her pale pink lipstick and hurried into the kitchen to finish her preparations for dinner. The past was over, and this was certainly no time to resurrect it.

Precisely one hour after Sarah had issued her reluctant invitation, two clean and well-pressed guests arrived on her doorstep. Tony's face in particular was almost shiny with soap and health. She wondered how long it had taken Brett to remove the accumulated grime of school and dogs. In any case he'd done a very good job. Her disturbing and disconcerting neighbor was obviously a conscientious father, which was one point in his favor, and even if he was a lousy cook she supposed he did the best he could.

He was looking more attractive than ever too, in superbly well-fitting gray trousers and a pale gray open-necked shirt which almost matched her new furniture. She wasn't sure if that was an improvement or not. At least with him in his worn corduroys and mud-caked hiking boots it had been easier to convince herself that her painstakingly constructed barriers against the male sex were well in place. Funny, though—this was the first time they had been even remotely threatened since the day she had first put them up.

Sarah only realized she was staring when her eyes encountered his and saw that his lips had lifted in a mocking, all too perceptive smile.

"Well? Will I do?" The smile was an open invitation now—an invitation she didn't trust one bit.

Oh, yes, he'd do, and he knew it. But she wasn't about to give him the satisfaction of hearing from her lips what she was sure he'd already read in her eyes.

"At least you're clean this time," she replied dampingly—and turned her attention to Tony. "What would you like to do while I get the supper on?" she asked him. "I've got lots of *National Geographics* you could look at and some books on model ship building. Or you could borrow my binoculars and watch the seabirds——"

"Can I watch TV?" Tony cut her off at the pass.

"TV? Yes, I suppose so. I only have a small set."

"It'll do," Brett interrupted dryly. "Size doesn't matter. As long as it's noisy and violent, my son will be quite content."

Sarah threw him a look of remote disapproval and went to switch on the set which sat unobtrusively on a small table in the corner.

"Aha," said Brett, when she returned to offer him a drink. "I see I've just been disqualified from the Father of the Year sweepstakes. Fathers who encourage noise and violence don't meet your standards of responsible paternity, do they?"

"Hardly," said Sarah primly, not sure whether she wanted to laugh or slap that look of provoking amusement off his face.

"Mmm," murmured Brett. "Well, let me tell you, if you had to spend twenty-four hours a day with an overactive, animal-mad nine-year-old with a predilection for noise, you'd know that anything which kept him in one place for half an hour couldn't be all that sinful."

"Maybe not," agreed Sarah, deciding in favor of laughter. "All the same, you're a fine one to talk about noise, Brett Jackson. And you're not with him twenty-four hours a day."

"At weekends," he amended. "And I only make noise in the mornings."

"How encouraging," she scoffed, handing him a drink as she headed into the kitchen. "So provided I'm in bed by ten o'clock like a good little girl, I can hope to catch a reasonable night's sleep, can I?"

Behind her she heard a low, sexy chuckle. "All depends what you mean by good, doesn't it?"

Sarah pursed her lips and swung through the door into the kitchen. Brett stretched himself as comfortably as was possible in the square, solid armchair, and studied her retreating figure with a speculative gleam in his eye. When she marched back into the room a short time later carrying a covered dish from which tantalizing aromas drifted, his expression sobered immediately as he rose to offer her a hand.

"It's all right," she said, still frosty. "Perhaps you can persuade Tony to leave the blood and gore for the time being. Supper's ready."

Brett raised his eyebrows, said nothing, switched off a scene of mob violence before which Tony sat entranced, and deposited his son, lower lip protruding mutinously, at the table.

"That was a good show, Dad," Tony started to protest. Then, as Sarah placed a plate of the steaming casserole in front of him, his expression changed and a small tongue emerged to make an anticipatory circle around his lips. "That smells *good*!" he exclaimed, starting to eat the minute he was told he could.

"A commendation not to be sneezed at," observed Brett. "I'd probably have served baked beans and eggs if put to it, but I had a feeling we'd do a bit better with you."

"Yeah," agreed Tony, licking a dollop of sauce off his cheek. "Dad usually makes macaroni and hamburgers. And fried chicken," he added, confirming Sarah's worst fears.

"Does he?" The frost had thawed from her voice now and she was smiling.

"Mmm, he's a great cook. But this is really great too." He sounded surprised. "What is it?"

Sarah laughed. "Trade secret," she told him.

Later, as she cleared away the crumbs that were all that was left of the casserole, she reflected that it had been a long time since she'd had anyone to dinner—apart from her parents. And, rather to her amazement, she had to admit she was enjoying it.

Brett was relaxed and appreciative now, not jeering or making unnecessary noise. And he was looking at her as if she was someone special. No one had looked at her like that for ages, and although it scared her in a way, threatened her hard-won security, it was nice to talk to a man who wasn't either Angela's client or some family friend she had known for most of her life.

Tony too, with his boundless energy, freckles and wide-eyed chatter, was an antidote for what she was just beginning to acknowledge might have been boredom.

After they had eaten dessert—blueberry pie which also earned approving murmurs—Tony returned to watch a very satisfactory shoot-out on TV which Brett immediately insisted he turn down. Then he and Sarah settled themselves with coffee at the other end of the long, uncluttered room.

"So," said Brett, stretching out legs that seemed to go on forever, "am I right in thinking you're a traveler, Sarah Malone?"

"A traveler?"

"Mmm. You enjoy new places and new faces, don't you? And you avoid putting down roots——"

"What on earth makes you say that?" asked Sarah, who had roots as deep as a mineshaft in Caley Cove, where her father had run the pharmacy long before she was born.

He waved a hand around the room and gestured at the models lining the walls. "All this. Good, but rather impersonal furniture. Easy to sell and not a lot of it. No frills——"

"You sound like my mother," interrupted Sarah.

"And everywhere I look I see ships," he continued, ignoring her. "And the sea outside the window. All symbols of escape to distant lands."

"Huh," snorted Sarah. "You may be a brilliant animal doctor, my friend, but as a clairvoyant you'd be put out of business in a week. Unless you consider Vancouver, Canada a distant land."

"Vancouver?" He shook his head. "No, I don't think so. A couple of hours' drive doesn't qualify."

"How about Seattle, then? Because that's as far as I've been."

"Is it? You surprise me."

"I don't see why."

He shrugged, and she wished he wouldn't because the movement emphasized the disturbing breadth of his shoulders.

"Okay, so I was wrong. You live in this spartan style because you like it, and the ships and the sea are merely a convenient—accident?"

"Hardly an accident. I build ships because I've always enjoyed the sea—and the vessels that sail on it. And I enjoy the detail that goes into putting my models together. I'm alone a lot and it gives me something to do."

As soon as the words were out of her mouth she knew they were a mistake, because Brett's legs seemed to grow even longer as he settled into the chair, smiled his slow, lazy smile and asked softly, and as though he had every right to know, "Why, Sarah? Why the navy blue armor? Who do you work so hard at being lonely?"

Sarah fought down the blush she felt starting on the soles of her feet, and was glad she hadn't turned the light on. Here, in the pale orange dusk, it was still possible to believe he couldn't see the effect his low voice was having on her emotions—his voice which was demanding an answer she didn't much want to give. Because he was making her face up to things she hadn't faced for years. And he was doing it while he sat opposite her, sprawled in her uncomfortable chair with his hands locked behind his head, and his golden eyes, dark now in the dim light from the window, appraising her in a way that seemed to see beneath her dress—navy blue armour, he had called it—to the soft, woman's body that had suddenly gone rigid with—what? Fear? Embarrassment? Desire? A little of all of them, perhaps.

But he was still sitting there, implacable, waiting for her to answer. She swallowed. "I—I didn't say I was lonely. I said I was alone a lot. There's a difference."

"Yes, sometimes. But not, I think, in your case."

Damn him. And he was right, of course. She had spent all these years building her barriers, convincing herself that she was happy—and in spite of that, all it had taken was one look from a pair of dark gold eyes, one soft question murmured in the autumn dusk, to rip away the veils of self-deception she had hidden behind for so long. Because she *was* lonely.

Yes, and she would stay lonely. It was the only way to save herself from being hurt again—maybe next time so badly it might destroy her. She couldn't take that. Not again.

He was still watching her, she knew, although his eyes were hooded now, shielded behind long dark lashes.

"Maybe I am lonely sometimes," she admitted, deciding that honesty, followed by a quick change of subject, was the best policy. "But I'm used to it, and my life's really quite comfortable. Also," she pressed on, determined to have everything quite clear, "you're not entirely wrong about the traveling. I had great plans once—to see India, China, Europe—oh, the whole world really. But I guess my—my dreams changed. Now, most of the time, I'm quite content to stay here."

"I see," said Brett, who saw rather more than she intended.

"Yes," she went on quickly. "It's a beautiful part of the world, isn't it? So peaceful. Nothing much happens here and that's the way I like it."

"Is it?" It was almost dark now, but she could tell from his tone that he didn't really believe her.

"Yes, of course it is. Perfect for dogs. And ferrets. That's what you said, isn't it?"

"You want to talk about dogs?" He wasn't so implacable now. In fact he sounded disbelieving.

"Why not?" She laughed nervously. At the moment she wanted to talk about anything that wasn't connected with herself.

"All right." Now she had a feeling he was smiling— a faintly cynical smile.

So they talked about dogs. Dogs that Brett and his brother had owned growing up in Seattle long before he opened his clinic on the Peninsula, dogs he had treated at the clinic, and the two obstreperous dogs called Sparky and Pickles who had been callously discarded by their former owner the moment they proved inconvenient.

And all the time they were talking, still almost in the dark, but with the TV chattering and flickering across the room, Sarah was conscious of something waiting to happen. Of Brett's firm, quiet voice soothing her, lulling her into a false sense of security which she sensed was a very temporary illusion. For how could there be security with a man like Brett so close to her, his large man's body a looming, hypnotic shape in the dusk?

She ran her tongue over her lips and jumped up quickly. But that proved the wrong thing to do because Brett stood up too and followed her into the kitchen.

"Running away?" he asked conversationally, as she switched on the light and flooded the small, compact room with a bright, fluorescent glare.

"No, of course not." She didn't look at him. "Putting on more coffee, that's all."

"We've already had two cups."

"Oh." Now she was forced to look at him. He was standing with his hands in his pockets, a stance which emphasized his thighs, and his head was bent toward her as he appeared to come to a decision.

In a moment she knew what that decision was, as suddenly he removed his big hands from his pockets and gripped them gently but firmly around her upper arms.

"What's the matter? What are you doing?" she gasped, all her muscles tightening at his touch.

"Nothing's the matter. But I never could resist a challenge. And you're certainly a challenge, Sarah Malone."

"What do you mean? I..." She stopped then because his left hand had circled behind her head and his firm, square-tipped fingers were tangled in the short, soft hair at her neck. Then his thumb began to stroke her skin, very slowly, just below her earlobe, sending shafts of shivering anticipation down her spine.

"Don't," she whispered. "Brett, please..."

"Why not? What are you afraid of, Sarah? I promise I don't bite. At least, not without an invitation."

Now his thumb was moving in feather-light circles,, teasing the base of her throat. Sarah closed her eyes, and as she did so she felt his warm, spiced wine breath against her cheek.

"Is that an invitation?" he asked softly.

Sarah opened her mouth to say no. But it was too late. The moment her lips parted, Brett closed them again with a kiss.

It wasn't a demanding kiss, but it was inescapable—probing and exploratory, giving as much as it took as his arms cradled her firmly against his chest. And for a moment Sarah felt she belonged there. She wasn't afraid of him after all and for the first time in—oh, so long—she felt secure, almost as if she was meant to be here, in the arms of this big, teasing male. Without really meaning it to happen, she raised her arms and placed them around his neck.

What might have happened next she never knew, because just as Brett's grip began to tighten around her a faint shuffling sound came from the open doorway, and then a high, boyish voice started to ask hopefully, "Sarah, d'you happen to have any pop I could——?"

The voice stopped abruptly, and then went on again after a loud, painfully disgusted sigh. "Dad! Why do you always kiss ladies in kitchens now? You never used to do that with Mom."

# CHAPTER THREE

BRETT'S arms loosened slightly, but they remained casually in place as he lifted his lips from Sarah's and glanced across at his son. Sarah, on the other hand, jerked as if she'd been doused with scalding water and dropped her hands like a child caught stealing cookies. But when she tried to push Brett away he wouldn't release her.

"Don't be embarrassed," he murmured from the corner of his mouth. And then to Tony, with an oddly enigmatic smile, "I'd have done the same with your mother if she'd let me. And I don't always kiss ladies in kitchens——"

"Yes, you do. There was Aunt Elise and then Mary-Jo Kry—Kry..."

"Krysenski. And that wasn't in a kitchen. It was——"

"Brett!" Sarah's voice rose in a crescendo, as the breath which had been knocked out of her on Tony's entrance returned in an indignant rush. "Brett, really! You've just been caught in a—a compromising position by your nine-year-old son, and instead of trying to repair the damage you're standing here bickering about where you usually kiss your—your *women!*" She poured a wealth of contempt into the word. "And now will you kindly let me go?"

Brett glanced down at her flushed and angry face, and in that instant Sarah saw a very odd expression distort his features. It was a look compounded of suspicion and a curious sort of rage, as if her words had done more than put a dent in his ego. As if, in some strange way, she had reminded him of something he had no wish to remember. And he was furious with her. Then he lowered his long lashes, and when he raised them again the anger had been concealed, and there was only patronizing mockery in his gaze.

"Aha. The return of the sweet old-fashioned girl," he drawled. "Compromising position, indeed. *Were* you compromised, Sarah?"

His voice was soft, purring like a satisfied cat, and Tony was still standing in the doorway staring from one to the other with a puzzled frown between his wide blue eyes.

"What's a compromising position?" he asked anxiously. "And what did my Dad damage, Sarah? I don't see any broken cups or chairs this time..."

"Oh!" Sarah suddenly found a strength she hadn't known she possessed, unclasped Brett's fingers which still rested lightly around her waist, and gave him an almighty shove in the stomach which sent him staggering back across the room.

"Atomic!" cried Tony admiringly. "You almost made him fly, Sarah. Are you Mrs. Superman, or something?"

"No," gasped Brett, obviously winded. "She's a fiend in female form. And as you can see, Sarah, my son's psyche is a great deal more resilient than you imagined. I assure you it won't be irreparably damaged by seeing you kissed."

"I don't think I've got a psyche, Dad," objected Tony. "My teacher would have told me if I had. Are you really a fiend, Sarah?" He returned to a subject of much more engrossing interest.

Sarah gave up. Maybe Tony was right and he didn't have a psyche. He certainly didn't look irreparably damaged. In fact he was positively glowing with ghoulish glee—at the prospect that she, Sarah, might be a fiend in human form.

"No," she replied, disillusioning him promptly. "I'm just a lady who made the mistake of letting your father talk her into cooking him dinner. Now, here's the pop you wanted——" she opened the fridge and handed him a can of orange drink "—and maybe you'd better go and watch some more TV. Your dad and I have to talk."

"Okay," said Tony obligingly, "but he'll probably try to kiss you again, you know."

"Oh, no, he won't," said Sarah, as Tony's small form departed jauntily in the direction of the living room.

"Oh, yes, he will," contradicted Brett, advancing across the kitchen toward her.

Sarah ran her tongue nervously over her lips. "Do you really break cups and chairs?" she asked, backing away from him.

It wasn't what she had meant to say at all but it had the effect of stopping him in his tracks. Now he reminded her of nothing so much as a tall, brooding statue of some old-time god, as he stood staring at her, tawny eyes unblinking and cool as pale gold glass.

"What is it?" she asked finally, when his silence and his curiously inward look began to alarm her. "What have I said?"

He moved then, shaking his head and smiling bleakly, as if, Sarah thought, he was making a conscious effort to shut out ugly images. "You haven't said anything," he told her. "But since you ask, yes, there was one occasion on which, I regret to say, I behaved like the proverbial bull in a china shop. Unfortunately Tony caught me—and wanted to join in."

"I don't doubt it," said Sarah, eyeing him warily. She had no difficulty whatever in imagining that a spot of enthusiastic, parentally sanctioned vandalism would be

near and dear to Tony's heart. But she didn't want Brett
to get any ideas about that sort of behavior being acceptable in *her* kitchen.

Apparently he read her mind.

"It's all right," he assured her. "I've been thoroughly
tamed since those days. I don't break crockery any
more."

No, thought Sarah involuntarily, noting the way the
corner of his lip curled upward in what looked to her
almost like a sneer. You just break hearts. And immediately all the recollections of her mother's rumors
about Brett's past—rumors which she had been trying
not to think about and hadn't wanted to believe—came
surging back. This man would never be tamed. Maybe
he didn't break things any more, but that was probably
because he always got his way. Men as appealing as Brett,
who oozed sensuality just by walking across a room or
raising a well-shaped eyebrow, usually did get everything—and every woman, they wanted. Tony, in his
bright innocence, had implied a long line of willing
women. Out of the mouths of babes...? She shook her
head, not knowing she was doing it. Brett had more or
less denied it, of course, but hadn't that denial been just
a little too glib? Too practiced, maybe? She didn't *want*
to believe the rumors. For a reason she couldn't begin
to understand, they hurt. But she, of all people, knew
the difference between illusion—believing what one
wanted to believe—and reality. That reality which had
taught her that an attractive and plausible package did
not necessarily conceal equally desirable contents.

Sarah closed her eyes briefly. Yes, she had known all
that, and yet she had been like putty in his arms a few
minutes ago, even though she knew practically nothing
about him.

He, on the other hand, knew that she lived alone, was probably lonely and bored and would therefore, to his mind, be an easy and convenient conquest. As she might have been if Tony hadn't come in when he did.

Brett was sitting with his hip resting on the edge of her chrome and white table now, looking relaxed and at ease as his smile tried to work its magic on her again.

"Sarah——" he began.

"You'd better go," she interrupted him, as angry with herself as she was with him.

"Hmm." He raised his eyebrows in just that way calculated to disturb her, and his fingers began to strum against his thigh. "Why, Sarah? Because I kissed you? You were going to kiss me back, you know. Or do I have to go because Tony saw us? He really doesn't mind, I assure you."

"I dare say he doesn't. I expect he's so used to seeing you 'kissing ladies in the kitchen' that he thinks it's the normal way for adults to behave. And I certainly *wasn't* going to kiss you back. You have a very inflated opinion of your own irresistibility, Brett Jackson. This is one lady who is not about to fall for your macho charms."

As she spoke, Brett stopped smiling and stood up. A light glinted in his eyes for a moment, pierced her like a sharp electric charge, and was replaced by a look of such deep, derisive and, in an odd way, pain-filled scorn, that she felt as if she'd been hit in the face with a knife.

But all he said, in a voice that held only a faint inflection of anger, was, "I see. As a matter of fact I thought kissing *was* a fairly normal way for adults to behave. But thank you. I suppose I should be grateful for your somewhat belated honesty. The fact of the matter is, of course, I'm not in the least grateful." Again the corner of his lip twisted in that unattractive curl. "You shouldn't send out misleading messages, Sarah. It may be an amusing little game to you, but one of these days some man is going to come along who won't be willing to play. And you may not enjoy the outcome. However, as my mother brought me up to be a gentleman, I'll go. Thank you for an excellent meal.''

Sarah gaped at him, speechless. That was no gentleman stalking away from her through the door, that was a barely controlled, very angry man whose gloriously sexual aura assaulted her senses with every swinging step he took.

Gloriously sexual? Had she really thought that?

She stared at his shoulders, at his long back and gray-sheathed hips and thighs. Yes, she had. There was no getting away from it, but——

At that moment her mesmerized musings were interrupted as Tony bounced in to thank her for the supper. He told her his dad said they had to check on the dogs and Fawcett now because they hadn't got properly used to the new house yet and might be lonely.

"Yes—yes, of course," mumbled Sarah. "I'm glad you enjoyed your supper."

She stood at the window and watched as the two of them walked hand in hand toward the gate—and to her disgusted irritation she found herself wondering if Brett's waving, glossy red-brown hair had been as blond as Tony's when he was young.

Then she brushed her own hair back in an unconscious effort to brush Brett out of her mind. But it didn't work. As she stacked the dishes in the dishwasher, slowly and with uncharacteristic heaviness, she couldn't banish the memory of his kiss. It had been so long since . . . and in any case Jason had never kissed her like that. Jason had been a taker, not a giver.

She shook her head. That made no sense, did it? Because surely Brett was a taker too? He had thought it would be a simple matter to take advantage of her proximity and aloneness. He had followed her into the kitchen with all the confidence of Farmer Mackenzie's prize bull in a field of willing cows. And broken china had not been in his mind at all.

Yes, argued another voice in Sarah's head, but he certainly didn't act like a prize bull. Not really. That kiss had been warm and sweet—and he was right. She had been about to return it.

She closed the lid of the dishwasher with a bang, tried to pour herself more coffee and discovered there wasn't any, muttered under her breath and marched out into the living room to think.

The moon was casting black shadows across the lawn as she sat down by the window and stared out into the night. With the television off she could hear the waves crashing against the cliffs far below. It was a lonely sound, empty and eternal. And it suited her mood.

Had she misled Brett? She'd been comfortable with him in a way, talking about dogs and his childhood, but still there had been that tension between them—a tension which she knew now had been caused by their physical closeness, by a hunger which she hadn't wanted to acknowledge. And of course he had been aware of it, tried to use it to satisfy his own needs. A man as virile as Brett probably had robust sexual appetites—as her mother's rumors seemed to bear out.

No, she decided, as a wave, larger than the others, reverberated loudly in the night. No, she hadn't misled him. It was just that he was so convinced he was irresistible to women that it had been a blow to his ego when she turned him down. His anger and accusations, which were in marked contrast to his usual easy confidence, had been sheer male chauvinism on the rampage. And it would do him good to know that there was at least one woman who *didn't* find him irresistible.

Sarah nodded her head emphatically, realized she was sitting in the dark and that she had to get to work in the morning, and headed purposefully in the direction of her bedroom—the bedroom that looked out at Brett's house.

She was particularly careful with the curtains, making sure that not even a chink of light showed between the ice-blue linen folds.

Sarah repeated this same performance every night for the remainder of the week, but as far as she knew she needn't have bothered. Not once did she catch even a glimpse of her new neighbor or his son, and, although the dogs greeted her noisily every evening, she only patted them hastily over the fence before making a beeline for her door—and safety from Brett's prying eyes. Not that he seemed to be remotely interested in prying, she admitted, annoyed with herself for feeling a half-formed regret. She also paid particular attention to the lock on her door these days, just in case Fawcett had discovered a new escape route. But there was no sign of the furry white Houdini.

By Saturday Sarah had come to the conclusion that Brett and his menagerie were not going to make any difference to her life after all. Not a sound had come from next door in the early hours of the morning and, as a result, she slept in until eleven o'clock.

At four o'clock she was still trying to catch up on her washing and housework before leaving for her parents' house at five. She was just piling the last load of wash into a white plastic laundry basket when she was startled by a tapping sound on her back door.

Funny, no one ever came to the back. It faced the cliffs and the sea, and wasn't easily accessible. But that noise certainly *sounded* like knuckles rapping on wood. Not very big knuckles either. Sarah glanced anxiously at her watch, closed the dryer and hurried out to investigate.

A small bare-footed figure, dressed in shorts and a mud-splashed T-shirt, stood on the narrow step staring up at her, his blue eyes as wide as saucers and filled with unshed tears.

"Tony! What are you doing here? And why didn't you come to the front?"

"I didn't want my Dad to see me."

"But why not?" Sarah pulled the door wider and beckoned him in.

He needed no second invitation. "Because I'm not talking to him. Ever again."

"Oh. Oh, dear." She closed the door quickly, wondering what on earth she ought to do with this small, very determined refugee with the jutting obstinate chin who suddenly reminded her forcibly of his father. "Um—why aren't you talking to him, Tony?" she asked doubtfully, not sure she really wanted to know.

"Because he took Fawcett to the clinic to have an operation and I didn't want him to. Then he said he'd take me to the Game Farm tomorrow, but now he's not going to." The tears had disappeared and been replaced by an impressively angry scowl.

"Oh, dear," said Sarah again. "Er—what's the matter with Fawcett?"

*"Nothing,"* replied Tony in tones of deep resentment. "There was nothing wrong with him at all. And now he's got *stitches* on his tummy and——"

"Stitches? I don't understand..."

"And it's not fair," continued Tony, ignoring the interruption. "Dad said Fawcett wasn't a baby any more and that he was getting frus-frustrated."

"Frustrated?" echoed Sarah faintly.

"Yes, just 'cos he was having a—a..." Tony screwed up his small face, searching for the word. "A *pashanut* affair," he brought out triumphantly. "That's what I heard him tell Aunt Elise. With Dad's running shoe. When Dad was in the shoe," he added, looking puzzled. "I don't know what he meant, though, do you?"

"I—um..." Sarah turned away and began to rummage frantically in the fridge.

"Do you, Sarah?" he persisted, when her head did not emerge again at once.

She gazed hopelessly at a jar of kiwi fruit jam bought in a moment of misguided curiosity. It didn't help. She was still trying desperately not to choke and fighting a losing battle to control her shaking shoulders.

"Sarah?" Tony's voice was beginning to sound accusing.

Making a superhuman effort, she took a deep breath, removed her nose from the jam, forced her shoulders back and took out a carton of apple juice. "Would you like a drink, Tony?" she asked in a strangled voice.

"Yes, please," he replied automatically, holding out his hand to accept it. "But, Sarah, you still haven't told me what Dad meant. About Fawcett and the pashanut affair."

Sarah groaned inwardly and took another, longer breath, mentally cursing Brett for the ineffectual way he was handling—or not handling—the matter of the birds and the bees.

"You go on into the living room," she said to her small guest now. "I'll be with you in just a minute."

"You're not going to phone my dad, are you?"

"No. At least not yet. I'm going to phone *my* dad."

"Okay." Satisfied, Tony padded out of the room, leaving Sarah to explain to her disbelieving parents that she'd be a little late for supper because she was entertaining a very young man.

She didn't really have much hope that Tony might have forgotten about Fawcett's problems when she went to join him a few minutes later—and he hadn't.

"*Now* tell me about Fawcett," he commanded.

"But didn't your father explain?" Sarah was stalling.

"No, but I think he was going to. Then Aunt Elise phoned just when we came back with Fawcett and after that Dad said he couldn't take me to the Game Farm after all. So I ran away."

"Yes, I see," said Sarah, wishing that his instinct for flight had driven him at least as far as the Mackenzies down the road, instead of only as far as her back door. "But surely your father saw you leave? Didn't he?"

"He was pulling Sparky out of the flowerbed she was digging up and I *snuck* out," Tony explained triumphantly.

"I see," said Sarah again, knowing full well she ought to be on the phone setting Brett's mind at rest, and at the same time thinking that a little worry would serve him right for disappointing Tony about the Game Farm—apparently in order to meet the mysterious Aunt Elise. The one he had kissed in a kitchen? Then she saw that Tony's lips were forming the inevitable question, and went on quickly, "About Fawcett. I think your father meant that he's a grown up ferret now and—he was having a—oh, dear—a passionate affair with—well, the point is, he doesn't have a wife. And that made him uncomfortable. So it was best for him to have the operation so he wouldn't be uncomfortable any more." She closed her eyes, praying desperately that that would be the end of the subject.

It wasn't.

"Dad doesn't have a wife either," her inquisitor pointed out. "Does that mean *he'd* be more comfortable too, if he had an operation?"

"I—I..." But Sarah, who was showing signs of imminent strangulation, was spared the necessity of answering. As her eyes snapped open again a harsh voice cracked through the open window.

"No, Tony, it does not. Although I suspect it might make *Sarah* more comfortable if Fawcett and I had that in common." He turned the full force of his eyes, glittering with malicious amusement, on the woman who sat gazing up at him, stunned and speechless.

"Now, Sarah, perhaps you'll be good enough to explain what you are doing with my son in *your* house— discussing passionate affairs."

# CHAPTER FOUR

SARAH gaped at him, her lips unconsciously parted, then she started to rise from her chair. But Brett moved suddenly and placed his hand above the window in a gesture that was peculiarly threatening—almost as if he was going to smash the glass and step inside to confront her, instead of making use of the door.

She swallowed and sank back against the pale gray fabric. "Won't—won't you come in?" she murmured, knowing quite well that he would certainly come in if he chose to, whether she invited him or not.

He didn't answer, just gave her a searching look and strode across the grass to the door. His fist was already pounding against the panels by the time she reached the small hallway and began to fumble with the lock she had been at such pains to secure.

"Well?" said Brett, brushing past her as if he owned the place, and swinging around to face her as she followed him into the room.

"Well what?" Sarah ran the tip of her tongue over her lips, unaware that the gesture made her look sexy and inviting.

He frowned and put his hands behind him on the windowsill. "Please don't pretend to be obtuse, Sarah. What are you doing with Tony, and what do you mean by discussing my...?" He hesitated.

"Personal business?" suggested Sarah hastily, before he could become more specific.

"Precisely. Extremely personal." His lips were not smiling. Neither were his eyes. But was that a quiver in his voice?

"Well, first of all, I didn't exactly kidnap Tony, he came on his own. And secondly, you were not the topic under discussion. Fawcett was." Sarah wished her face weren't turning crimson, but she couldn't honestly imagine that any woman would be capable of standing here staring into Brett's manly face and discussing that particular business without producing at least a minor blush.

"All right, I suppose I have to accept that," he conceded. "In spite of my son's somewhat unnerving suggestion." He regarded her pink cheeks reflectively.

"What suggestion?" Tony, who up until then had been sitting by the window scowling, found that natural nosiness was forcing him to acknowledge his father's existence.

Reluctantly, Brett removed his gaze from Sarah's face to concentrate on the ceiling. "Never mind. We'll talk about it afterward. We'll also discuss Fawcett in private."

"But Sarah was just starting to explain——"

"I said we'll talk about it later." The tone of his voice brooked no argument, and Tony, lower lip protruding sulkily, subsided into a chair and began to kick his left foot rhythmically against the wall.

"Stop that at once," said Brett sharply.

Tony stopped, and his father glared down at him, shaking his head. He looked baffled now as well as exasperated and Sarah felt a sudden stab of sympathy for this tough but by no means perfect man. Brett obviously tried to be a good father, but, as he had pointed out himself, coping with an over-active, animal-mad nine-year-old wasn't exactly a bed of roses. Or, if it was, she was willing to bet they were exceptionally prickly ones.

"It's all right," she said quietly. "My walls are fairly solid."

"So I've noticed, but that's no excuse for abusing them."

"No, I suppose not, but I think..." Her voice trailed off.

"What do you think, Sarah?"

That lazy, curling note was stirring her insides again, and she stepped away from him quickly. "I think Tony's upset about more than Fawcett. He says you were going to take him to the Game Farm——"

"I was, but something's come up and I've had to change my plans. Life's full of disappointments, and the sooner Tony learns to accept that, the better." He spoke harshly, and there wasn't even a hint of understanding on his face. Understanding for a small boy who was very naturally upset about the cancellation of a promised treat—because his father had more important business to see to. A flash of anger shook Sarah then that was out of all proportion to its cause. A cause called Elise who happened to be the "something" that had come up.

"That's not fair, Brett," she snapped at him. "Of course Tony's disappointed. He's only a kid. And he ought to come before your—your assignations."

"Assignations? What the hell are you talking about?"

"'Aunt' Elise," replied Sarah, her soft voice dripping gentle acid.

"Ah. I see." He had his hands in his pockets now and was rocking back on his heels as a small, malicious smile twisted his lips.

"What do you see?" asked Sarah suspiciously.

"Don't you know?" His eyes flicked over her sharply. "No, perhaps you don't. In that case I do believe I perceive signs of a quite promising jealousy. How flattering. Especially as I'd almost given up hope."

"Oh," cried Sarah, her brown eyes narrowing. "Oh! You unspeakably smug, conceited, vain, self-satisfied..."

"Chauvinistic?" he suggested, lifting his eyebrows infuriatingly as she struggled in vain for words.

"Yes, that too." She glared at him. "Not to mention abominably stupid. Why should any woman be jealous over you? Egocentric jerks aren't in style."

To her increasing fury, Brett only smiled complacently. He was spared the necessity of answering though when Tony, distracted from his ill-humor, asked interestedly, "Are you going to kiss her again, Dad? You always end up kissing Aunt Elise after she yells at you."

Brett brushed his hand across his mouth. "I don't think so," he replied dryly. "I have a healthy respect for my own skin—which I suspect might get sadly scratched if I tried to kiss this particular pussycat. Besides..." he paused and then went on lightly "...it's been quite some time now since I kissed Aunt Elise—whether she was yelling at me or not."

"An omission which will soon be remedied," muttered Sarah, before she could stop herself.

"I doubt it," said Brett shortly.

Sarah shrugged and said nothing.

"Not that it's any of your business," he added.

"No," she agreed coldly. "Tony wasn't my business either until he came running over here for comfort because you'd let him down."

Brett's jaw tightened. "I did *not* let him down," he growled at her. "I'm fulfilling an obligation to an old friend who used to be my receptionist and needs my help moving tomorrow. Her current boyfriend has broken off their engagement as well as his promise to move her. But don't worry, Tony will get his trip to the Game Farm. Next weekend."

"But it may be raining by then," objected Tony, with deep and not unfounded pessimism. It had been hot and sunny for so long that the rains of autumn couldn't be far away.

"Well, we'll just have to take our chances, won't we?" said Brett, who now sounded more weary than impatient.

Sarah heard the weariness and, to her surprise and annoyance, the sympathy she had felt earlier returned.

"I'll take Tony tomorrow," she heard herself saying. "That is, if you'll let me."

"Don't be ridiculous. Why should you?"

"Why shouldn't I? I don't have more important plans," she informed him tightly and with a slight emphasis on the pronoun. "And Tony's right. It may very well be raining next weekend."

"No. It's out of the question."

"Dad!" wailed Tony from the window. "Dad, that's not fair."

Brett ran a distracted hand through his hair. "Life's rarely fair, Tony," he said tiredly.

"But it ought to be," insisted his son. "Sarah says she doesn't mind."

"Oh, Lord," Brett muttered under his breath. "Do you always have to complicate things, Sarah?"

"I thought I was simplifying them," she replied, sinking stiffly onto the arm of a chair and not looking at him.

"Yes, I suppose you did." He sounded bemused again—bemused and very much as if he wished he were anywhere else but here, in her living room, trying to convince her and his son—and perhaps himself—that her perfectly reasonable solution to his problem was not reasonable at all.

"Please, Dad," persisted Tony, sensing that the rock who was his parent was gradually being worn down.

Brett's broad shoulders shifted restlessly under his dark blue T-shirt. "All right," he said finally. His amber-gold eyes met Sarah's and she thought they seemed curiously flat. "All right. I see I'm outnumbered. You can have him if you want him, Sarah."

"Thanks," said Sarah bitingly. "How generous of you."

"Sorry." He smiled thinly. "That was hardly a gracious acceptance of your kindness, was it?"

"Not noticeably. But then grace isn't one of your more obvious charms."

"Thank you."

"Don't mention it."

She saw that Tony was watching them disapprovingly, and for the first time it occurred to her that no part of this unsuitable conversation should have taken place in front of Brett's son.

"Do you always conduct your arguments in front of Tony?" she asked him, arching her eyebrows.

"Believe it or not, hardly ever. Except, it seems, where you happen to be concerned."

"Mmm. Charming as ever, I see. And now, if you don't mind, I was supposed to be at my parents' house fifteen minutes ago..."

He nodded quickly. "Of course. Come on, Tony, Sarah's had enough of us for one day."

When they reached the door, after arranging that Brett should bring Tony over at ten, he turned suddenly, gave her that melting smile that had so captivated her from the start and said, "Thanks, Sarah. Believe it or not, I do appreciate your help. However, after our last rather—acerbic—meeting, it hardly seemed right to take advantage of your offer. A less than neighborly distance seemed more appropriate. Oh, and by the way——" he rested his shoulder casually against the doorframe

"—for your information I'm neither a chauvinist nor abominably stupid. It's just that you're the most provoking woman I've ever met—and I rather enjoy provoking you back." The smile turned into a mocking white grin as he touched her lightly on the cheek, put his hand on Tony's head, and strolled down the path to the gate with an easy, unhurried walk that made Sarah want to throw something at his back.

Oh! she thought, as she watched them go. Of all the nerve! Who did he think he was to talk about provoking? He'd come bounding in here and practically accused her of abducting Tony, then he'd had the gall to suggest she was actually jealous of his receptionist, and on top of that he'd bitten her head off for making a perfectly well-intentioned offer to help him with his son. And he dared to call her provoking. She'd give him provoking, she'd...

Hold it, Sarah, the voice of reason echoed in her mind. Just hold it. You're not giving him anything, my girl. You're taking Tony to the Game Farm tomorrow because you said you would and because you don't want a little boy to be disappointed—but certainly not because you want to do Brett Jackson any favors—and that will be the end of that. After tomorrow his "less than neighborly distance" will be maintained. Strictly.

She marched into the bedroom, nodding her head assertively, pulled on a clean pair of trousers after folding her dusty jeans into a hamper, gave herself a quick wash and hurried out to the car.

Yes, definitely less than neighborly, she decided as she drove at precisely the speed limit along the quiet road leading into town. There was no way she intended to provide a baby-sitting service in the future, just so that her arrogant neighbor would be free to pursue his amorous inclinations with "Aunt" Elise.

"You look all hot and bothered, dear," said her mother the moment she stepped over the threshold. "Not that man next door again, surely?"

Sarah wasn't certain whether her mother was expressing hope or disapproval. Normally it would be hope, but in this case the man in question was the subject of delectable rumors. At least that had been the case last weekend . . .

"Not really," she replied, flinging a pale blue sweater over the back of Clara's brightly flowered couch. "He came over to fetch Tony just as I was leaving, and that made me later than ever. So I've been rushing. I expect that's why I look a bit harried." She smiled brightly, because she had no intention of telling her mother more than that. If she did, Clara would either have her married off immediately or else be convinced that Brett was out to do her daughter harm. Which way the ball bounced would depend, of course, on the status of the latest rumors . . .

"Why? Did you hear something else about him, then?" she asked offhandedly, as the three of them sat down to eat baked ham.

Clara shook her head. "No," she replied. "It's very frustrating. Apparently now no one's quite sure if his wife really did commit suicide—and that receptionist of his—Elise somebody—well, it's possible they weren't having an affair——"

"How disappointing," murmured George Malone.

"Now, George, really . . ." Clara launched into a long, emphatic and unconvincing speech explaining that she wasn't actually interested in gossip, *but* . . .

Sarah let her eyes glaze over. So Tony's Aunt Elise was, in fact, the fatal receptionist. The one who had lured Brett from his loving wife . . . No. Not likely. Those tawny eyes of his were definitely of the roving variety and he probably hadn't needed any luring. For a moment her mind drifted, sympathizing with Tony's unfortunate mother, who had never even seen her child grow up. What had she been like, that unhappy woman from Brett's past? Beautiful and sad, enduring her husband's infidelities with resignation? Or had she been a fighter, tough and resilient until life had become too hard to bear? If that was the case, what was she, Sarah, doing aiding and abetting Brett in a liaison which had broken another woman's heart—as her own had once been broken? Assuming the rumors were true, of course, and she was becoming increasingly convinced that they might be, even as her mother's information became more vague. On the other hand, of course, they might be a complete fabrication...

"Idiot," she muttered under her breath.

"What, dear?" Clara immediately interrupted her own speech to turn an eagle eye on her daughter.

"Nothing," mumbled Sarah. "Just something I forgot to tell Angela at work."

Well, it wasn't *really* a lie. She *had* forgotten to tell Angela that the man from the Tax Department had called and would be calling again on Monday.

"Hmm." Clara had her suspicions but she didn't pursue the subject.

An hour later, rather earlier than usual because Tony would be arriving at ten, Sarah took leave of her parents and drove home to a house grown surprisingly cold.

By ten-fifteen the next morning there was still no sign of Brett or Tony. By ten-thirty she had given up expecting them and was mentally boiling Brett in oil for changing his mind about her offer and not even having the courtesy to let her know.

Muttering under her breath, she had just sat down at her modeling table to attach a particularly critical belaying pin to the rail of a scale model of Nelson's *Victory* when she heard small fists clattering on the door and Tony's excited voice shouting, "We're here, Sarah! Fawcett escaped again, and guess where we found him?"

As the noise had caused Sarah to drop the all-important pin, at that moment she rather wished they hadn't found the errant ferret. But she didn't say so, because when she opened the door and looked down into Tony's eager face she was surprised to feel a funny little tug inside her chest. The solitary precision of her hobby didn't seem so important any more.

"I'm sorry we're late," said Brett, who was standing beside his offspring with the morning sun polishing his hair to a burning copper. "Fawcett got out again. We found him in the downstairs bathroom demolishing rolls of toilet paper and a bar of deodorant soap."

"You didn't let her guess, Dad," grumbled Tony.

But Brett, judging from his compressed lips and the rigid way his muscles strained beneath his soft gray sweatshirt, was forcing himself to keep his temper. "I'm in no mood for guessing games," he said curtly, "and I very much doubt if Sarah is either."

"Bad morning?" she inquired sympathetically, as her irritation evaporated.

"You could put it that way."

"Yeah, Sparky dug a hole in the rug and Pickles ate Dad's clean underwear," chimed in Tony with glee.

"None of which would have happened if you had left the dogs outside as I told you, and put Fawcett in his cage—as I also told you." Brett's face was grim. "And if I didn't feel it would be unfair to an old friend to inflict you on her on moving day when I don't have to, I can assure you that you would *not* be going to the Game Farm."

"So you're inflicting him on me instead," said Sarah dryly, at the same time making a determined effort to keep her mind off the matter of Brett's recently digested underwear.

"You asked for it," he responded rudely. Then as Sarah opened her mouth to tell him what she thought of boorish, ungrateful men like him, he held up his hand and added shortly, "All right. I take it back. You're the answer to a prayer and I'm an ungrateful bastard."

He didn't sound repentant, though, he sounded abrupt and bad-tempered, and as he strode toward the large van parked at the side of the road and then sped off toward Port Angeles and his Elise Sarah wasn't altogether sure she blamed him.

She wasn't sure what she'd let herself in for either.

As it turned out, the expedition was a qualified success. Tony, delighted to be spending the day among bigger and better animals, behaved as well as he was able. Sarah soon discovered that this wasn't very well at all, but she enjoyed his enthusiasm, in spite of the fact that in order to keep him out of trouble she could have used at least four arms as well as two extra pairs of eyes. She had not visited the Farm herself since Lloyd Beebe had first opened it as a refuge for some of Walt Disney's retired animal stars, and she found that she shared Tony's delight in meeting the bears, wolves, cougars, wildcats and a host of other old friends from the movies. Funny, she felt surprisingly close to this little boy she had known for such a short time. This little boy, she reminded herself, who belonged to that large, annoying and impossibly attractive man next door.

All the same, at the back of her mind she was aware of a growing discontent with her existence. A discontent that hadn't been there before. A feeling that a life devoid of children of her own, and lived among model ships and bare, functional furniture, was not really any life at all.

Then, as she pulled Tony's clutching fingers off a cage containing a baleful-looking wolverine, and immediately afterward dissuaded him from climbing a tall wire fence, she decided that, on second thoughts, childlessness had its advantages—and again felt a wave of unwilling sympathy for Brett.

Which was why, when Tony suggested they drive up to Hurricane Ridge on the way home, she agreed readily. She had assured Brett they would be home by seven o'clock at the latest, but she didn't imagine he'd be anxious to see them much sooner—and according to her watch there would be plenty of time to take in a quick walk in the alpine meadows and still be home in time for supper.

The drive up the winding mountain road took a little longer than she expected, but she felt no sense of urgency as they walked around one of the shorter trails through the trees before making their way back to the car park perched almost a mile above the sea south of Port Angeles.

There would have been no urgency either, if her ancient but normally reliable Volkswagen had not waited until she attempted to start the engine before staging a full-scale strike.

Tony fastened his seatbelt and Sarah turned the key confidently as she gazed through the windshield at the soft shapes of the clouds brushing the glacier-covered slopes of the Olympics. She smiled. It was windy and fresh up here, bracing and beautiful...

And her engine wasn't turning over.

She closed her eyes and tried again.

"What's the matter?" asked Tony interestedly.

"The car won't start."

"Oh. Does that mean we'll be late?"

"Probably."

"Dad'll be mad." It was said more in anticipation of exciting parental fireworks than in trepidation. But then, why should he worry? She was the one responsible for their safe return.

She was about to swear rather pointedly, but Tony was staring at her, so she gave a few disgruntled growls beneath her breath instead.

"Can I help?" asked a tall young man with glasses who was parked beside them.

Sarah thought he looked the type who would be more at home conducting a seminar on accounting than fixing engines, but she supposed he couldn't know less about cars than she did—although she *could* change a tire in a pinch.

She accepted gratefully.

To her everlasting relief and surprise, the young man turned out to be a mechanic. So much for preconceptions about glasses, she chided herself.

Half an hour later he emerged from beneath the hood beaming with triumph.

"Oh, thank you," cried Sarah. "You've really saved our bacon."

"Glad to be of service," he replied, running his eyes appraisingly over her jeans and pale cream sweater.

"Um—yes. Can I offer you something for——?"

"Maybe," he drawled, his lingering gaze leaving her in no doubt about his meaning.

"Something financial," she finished quickly.

At that the young man laughed and shook his head, so Sarah thanked him again and beat a hasty retreat to her car. A few minutes later she and Tony were swerving down the twisting road to civilization.

At seven-thirty precisely, they swerved up in front of Sarah's house.

Tony unbuckled his seatbelt and jumped out.

Sarah switched off the engine and followed him more slowly as, over the noise of dogs barking and Tony's shouts of greetings to his furry friends, Brett's deep voice rolled out like a clap of malevolent thunder.

"Well, well, well. So you've decided to come home, have you, Sarah?"

As Sarah looked up into golden eyes that flicked over her like summer lightning, he added bitingly, "I suppose it would have been too much trouble to phone?"

# CHAPTER FIVE

"WHAT?" Sarah gaped at the dark, explosive face looming above her. Brett's color had deepened to a glowing bronze and those incredible eyes of his were glittering daggers of accusation. "What do you mean, Brett? I told you we'd be back around seven and it's only seven-thirty now."

"Oh, it's only seven-thirty, is it?" he said unpleasantly. "And I suppose it didn't occur to you that I might be concerned about Tony? I left Elise with a kitchen full of broken glass to clear up, rushed home in case you were early—and have spent the last hour and fifteen minutes wondering what in hell you'd done with my kid." He curled a large hand over the top of the gate, took a step toward her and pinned her against the fence so that she couldn't move without pressing against his chest.

Sarah, her senses reeling from his closeness and from the unexpected ferocity of his attack, fought down a burning urge to slap him. But she was not going to behave like an uncontrolled adolescent just because he was masquerading as a gorilla. No, that wasn't right, was it? Gorillas were supposed to be peaceful animals, and there was nothing remotely peaceful about this giant who was glowering down at her and looking for all the world like a pagan god bent on revenge. Violence quivered in the air around him and the only intelligent thing to do was defuse it.

"I'm sorry you were worried, Brett," she said coolly— very coolly. "But don't you think you're overreacting? Contrary to this obsession of yours, I have no desire whatever to kidnap your son. The fact is, my car broke down at the top of Hurricane Ridge, and it hardly seemed fair to leave the *nice* young man who was trying to help us——'' she laid particular stress on the word ''nice'' ''—in order to make a quite unnecessary phone call. At that point I still expected to be back by seven.''

Brett made a sound that was a cross between a snort and a crack of scornful laughter. ''I see. And when you discovered you wouldn't be? I suppose then it didn't seem worth the bother.''

''As we were stuck in a traffic jam at the time, no, it didn't. I got home as quickly as I could.''

''No, you didn't,'' interrupted Tony aggrievedly, breaking away from the clamoring dogs to add fuel to this very promising fire. ''You wouldn't break the speed limit, Sarah. We'd have got home much faster if you had.''

Brett turned away from Sarah to direct a look of acute disfavor at his son, who grinned with overplayed guilelessness and scuttled back to his dogs.

Sarah bent her head to hide her amusement. Brett's expression was a study in conflict. Conflict between his desire to tell her off for not hurrying, and the knowledge that he could hardly condemn her for obeying the law. She didn't dare look at him now because she knew that if she did she would inevitably give way to laughter—which would only antagonize him further.

Brett glared at her meekly bowed head with the hair curling rebelliously on her neck. ''If you kept that heap of yours in decent repair, there wouldn't have been any problem,'' he growled, hitting on another reason to berate her. ''Anyway, what the devil were you doing on Hurricane Ridge?''

He was still much too close and when she raised her eyes she could almost count the pores on his skin. ''I was trying to do you a favor, by giving you as much time on your own as possible," she told him, amusement giving way to indignation. "And if you must know, I keep my car in excellent repair. The man who helped us said having a choke stuck can happen to anyone. But I'll be getting it checked at the garage just to be sure." She lifted her chin and stared frigidly over his shoulder.

"Hmm."

Sarah stole a covert glance at his face. That "hmm" had sounded slightly less belligerent than before, and although his jaw still protruded aggressively she thought she detected a hint of doubt in his eyes.

"Now, if the inquisition is *quite* over," she continued acidly, "I'd be obliged if you'd move out of my way."

"Inquis... Oh, hell." He stepped back so abruptly that Sarah almost fell over, and to her amazed irritation she discovered she felt a certain regret that his large and threateningly powerful body was no longer preventing her escape.

"Good evening, Brett," she said, playing her role of ice maiden to the hilt as she swept past him to push open the gate.

The only answer she received was another grunt—and something which didn't sound printable.

It was almost ten o'clock when the knock came, a discreet, almost tentative knock this time, and Sarah groaned. She was already in her robe and slippers, and just putting the finishing touches to a ratline she was adding to a sail. The last thing she needed now was a visitor.

Sighing, she stood up, walked out into the hall and opened the door.

"Bloody little fool. You didn't even ask who was here. I could have been your friendly neighborhood rapist."

Brett was leaning against the doorframe with his arms crossed, and although he looked quite friendly now he didn't look much like a rapist.

Sarah pulled uselessly at the belt on her pale blue robe and hastily dismissed a wayward reflection that, if one had to encounter a pervert on a dark night, one could do worse than Brett Jackson.

"No, you couldn't," she countered. "He won't be out of jail for four years."

Brett shook his head disbelievingly. "Idiot," he murmured, his voice all velvet warmth now. "But you really should be more careful."

"Oh, should I? Well, let me tell you, so far the only man I've had cause to worry about around here has been *you*. I thought you were about to eat me earlier. Where's Tony?"

"Mrs. Mackenzie is sitting with him for a while. And I'm sorry about earlier. As for eating you—I'd like to. But I promise I'll keep my teeth to myself." He pulled back his lips to expose all the teeth in question in a leeringly wolfish grin.

In spite of herself, Sarah couldn't help grinning back.

"You look much more human when you smile," he observed carelessly. "You should do it more often, Snow Queen."

Sarah immediately stopped smiling and scowled instead.

"Good grief. The return of the fiend," he groaned. "I've put my foot in it again, haven't I? May I come in?"

"What for?"

"Because you must be getting cold standing there in that flimsily seductive bit of silk. And I want to talk to you."

"How do you know I want to talk to you?" she demanded, not trusting him at all now that he was talking about seduction.

"I don't. But sooner or later you'll have to, so we might as well make it now."

"Do you *always* get your own way?" she asked frostily, still not standing aside to let him in.

"No, but I intend to this time." With startling swiftness he placed both hands around her waist and lifted her back into the hall.

As soon as they were across the threshold he kicked the door shut behind him.

"Now," he said, releasing her to turn her around and propel her into the living room, "let's get down to business."

Sarah tightened her belt again and pulled the folds of her robe hastily over her chest.

Brett's lips twitched. "No, not that kind of business," he assured her. "Although the prospect is not unappealing." He nodded at the blue silk robe which molded the long, willowy lines of her figure. "That delightfully feminine garment is a great improvement on the armor, Sarah. You ought to wear it all the time."

"I doubt if my boss would appreciate it," she snapped.

"Then he's a fool."

"*She* is hardly a fool," retorted Sarah. "She's a remarkably intelligent woman."

"Ah. Of course. The redoubtable Ms. Baddeley. I'd forgotten."

Sarah felt the exasperation which was never far from the surface when she was around this man begin to bubble up inside her and boil over. "If all you disturbed me for was to discuss my wardrobe, Brett..."

"It wasn't, and I'm sorry I disturbed you. But there are some things that need to be said."

"Then please say them and get out." Sarah forgot about keeping herself covered and put both hands on her hips to convince him and herself that she meant exactly what she said.

Brett, a slow smile playing across his face, lowered himself onto the arm of a chair so that his eyes were on a level with her chest, and let his gaze wander appreciatively over the cleavage now exposed above her low-cut summer nightgown.

"I came to apologize," he said, draping an arm along the back of the chair, throwing his head back and giving her a not very penitent smile.

"Very well. Apology accepted. *Now* get out."

"Ouch." Brett winced. "Don't you want to know why I'm apologizing?"

"Not in the least. However, I imagine it has something to do with that disgraceful display of rudeness and bad temper you treated me to earlier this evening."

He winced again. "You don't pull your punches, do you? But of course you're right. It was a disgraceful display of bad temper, and I'm sorry."

Sarah eyed him doubtfully. He did look a little remorseful, but so far she had had very little reason to believe he gave a damn about her feelings. Besides, in her experience, most men were out to make things comfortable for themselves. And no doubt a handy babysitter who could also be prevailed upon to cook was a convenience too useful to be discarded lightly.

All the same, it was tempting—he was tempting, sitting there sprawled across her chair with his golden and— yes, definitely bedroom eyes fixed on her with that disarmingly seductive warmth. It would be so easy to melt into those eyes, to forgive him anything—including bursts of inexcusable temper...

"I've already said I accepted your apology," she said sharply, and before the eyes could wreak further havoc. "Now please go."

Brett shrugged. "If you insist," he said lightly, rising with unhurried grace to his feet.

But instead of leaving he moved toward her, pulled her left hand off her hip and took it firmly between his own tough palms. "Sarah, I realize you're not interested in excuses, and normally I don't make them." He smiled wryly. "However, as nothing else has been normal about today, I'll make an exception."

"Big of you," muttered Sarah, wanting to pull her hand away but discovering that the will to move had deserted her. "I'm really not interested, Brett."

"And I don't care if you're interested or not," he retorted, discovering that his already inadequate supply of patience was wearing thin. "I want to apologize to you and I intend to do it properly. That means an explanation."

"Translate: excuse," muttered Sarah sarcastically.

"If you like. Listen, young lady, if you'd had a day like the one I've had, even you might admit that there was some excuse for my having a short fuse this evening."

"Was it that bad?" she asked, curious in spite of herself, and seduced by the tingling warmth of his hands.

"Worse. It started with Tony encouraging those damn dogs to mount an assault on my carpets and my——"

"Yes, I know," she interrupted hastily.

The corner of his lip turned up, but he went on determinedly, "And that fiendish furball guzzling up our bathroom supplies. Of course after that I was late getting to Elise's place and she gave me hell. Then I spent an exhausting and extremely frustrating day moving the accumulation of ten years' worth of her pack-ratting from one end of Port Angeles to the other. In my station wagon. And she refused to throw out a damn thing. Some kid she knows who was supposed to be helping out didn't show up, so there were just the two of us—mainly me—and ten thousand boxes of useless junk. When she told me I had to load up three decayed rubber plants and a dead begonia—I blew up. We had one hell of a fight and I accidentally dropped a carton of glasses—which of course I'll have to replace—onto my foot. At that point I left, managed to acquire a speeding ticket on the way home—and then waited an hour and fifteen minutes for my son and his chaperon to arrive. As you saw, by that time I was ready to chew up knives. But as you were much more readily digestible, I chewed up you instead. *Not* an excuse for my behavior, I agree, but perhaps you'll accept that it is at least an explanation."

He was still holding her hand, standing very close to her, and smiling down with such rueful regret that Sarah had to conquer an urge to hold her free hand to his cheek and assure him that of course he was the blameless injured party and therefore entirely forgiven.

He must have read something of the sort in her eyes, because suddenly he caught hold of her other hand and said solemnly, "Can you forgive me, Sarah? For being an incredibly ungrateful bastard?"

Sarah's shoulders sagged. What was the use? It was impossible to stay angry when he looked at her like that, and anyway—her lips started to curl up—he had had a very bad day.

"Did—your friend—really ask you to move a dead begonia?" she asked, her voice quivering.

"And three dead rubber plants," he assured her morosely. "You don't know Elise."

No, she didn't, and it occurred to her that she didn't much want to.

But Brett had heard the laughter in her voice, and now he grinned and said with maddening assurance, "So you see, you'll have to forgive me."

"I don't see why."

"You want me to grovel, don't you? Well, I'm not going to."

"How disappointing," Sarah murmured, trying very hard not to smile.

"Isn't it. On the other hand, I did promise you a meal when I got some supplies in, and I would like to make amends. Tony's staying with a friend in town for a couple of nights next weekend. So will you accept my hospitality on Friday, Sarah Malone?"

"Who's doing the cooking?" she asked suspiciously.

His eyes widened. "Would I invite you to dinner and then expect you to make the meal?" he asked, all wounded innocence.

"Very probably."

He laughed. "You don't miss much, do you, Snow Queen? And as I see there's no help for it, I can manage a nice line in fried chicken. Will you come?"

Fried chicken. She'd known it. But, feeling as though she were being borne along by a particularly relentless tide, she was just about to accept when she had a sudden, unexpected vision of his wife, her face vague and blurry, staring wistfully out of a window—waiting.

"I—don't know," she muttered.

Brett's eyes narrowed. "Still scared of me?" he taunted. "I suppose you've heard that I eat dark-eyed virgins for dessert. Do you always believe everything you hear?"

That did it. "Of course I'm not scared of you," she scoffed, at the same time wondering if the reference to her chastity implied a question. If it did, it was a question she was not about to answer. "All right. I'll come," she agreed grudgingly. "Thank you."

"Don't look so enthusiastic," he said dryly. "My cooking isn't fatal, I promise."

Sarah wasn't so sure about that, because at that moment he dropped her hands and one of them brushed against his thigh. As she pushed it hastily into the pocket of her robe it seemed for a second as if everything about this man was fatal.

Then she was certain of it. His lips curved knowingly and to her stunned consternation he reached out to grasp her shoulders. She could feel his warmth through the thin blue silk as he pulled her in slow motion toward him. Her breasts were just touching his chest. She gasped, waiting for the inevitable—and Brett bent his head and dropped a feather-light kiss on her forehead.

"Good night, Sarah. See you on Friday around seven. And thank you. I know no woman in her right mind would set out to kidnap Tony."

The door closed softly and she heard his feet crunch on the gravel. Her eyes wide as an owl's, Sarah moved stiffly back to the table where she had been sitting when he arrived. She gazed blankly at the still unfinished ratline and shook her head in disbelief.

What an anticlimax! There she had stood, waiting for violent seduction, or worse—and all he had done was kiss her dismissively, as a father might kiss his child. On the forehead. And the most disturbing thing of all was that for one mad moment she had felt an overwhelming disappointment.

She shook her head again and wandered into her bedroom, still walking like a sleepwalker, oblivious to her surroundings. Then, as soon as she opened the curtains wider, she realized she had meant to close them.

"You're going crazy, Sarah," she whispered, as she moved back across the room.

For a long time before she got beneath the covers that night, she sat on the edge of the bed and stared blindly at the stark white walls.

What was happening to her? Life had been so simple, so well-ordered—but ever since Brett had come into it her safe, comfortable world had changed. She was no longer quite so sure that all she wanted was peace and solitude and a good, safe, predictable job. He was making her think differently about all the things she had considered important, like security and not getting involved—and remaining celibate. Yet here she was, half regretting a passionate interlude that hadn't happened and agreeing to have dinner with the cause of all her doubts. With the only man in ten years who had come close to breaching her carefully constructed defenses. A man who, she was very much afraid, was capable of making her feel again. Feel like a woman?

She shivered then and at last climbed into bed. Because she didn't want to feel. Feeling meant hurting. She knew all about that. It also meant excitement, sensation, fulfilment, love and sensuality. She knew all about that too, but it wasn't worth it. Not when in the end she was bound to lose it again.

In the case of Brett, she mused, forcing herself to concentrate on the root of her current problem, she wouldn't even gain much to lose. Oh, a nice little roll between the sheets, perhaps. Brett hadn't left her in much doubt that he'd be willing to oblige in that line. But he wouldn't even pretend to offer more. He'd made no bones about the fact that he was seeing Elise again, the woman who had quite possibly destroyed his marriage. She supposed she should be thankful for that. Brett might be short-tempered sometimes, and impatient, but at least he appeared to be honest.

But as the week passed and she went into work every day, and Angela studied the pouches under her eyes with growing concern, Sarah kept thinking that when Friday came she would be able to accept that honesty was just not enough. Then she would break the arrangement for dinner, and retreat forever behind her nice, safe, chilly walls.

Friday came, and with it, at last, the rain. Then seven o'clock came, and Sarah, still wearing her brown suit, sat by the window staring at the gray, relentless drizzle.

At seven-fifteen, as her fingers twisted the corner of a square white cushion, she looked up to see Brett, clad only in a striped shirt and trousers, striding aggressively up the path through the rain. He saw her at the same moment, and quickened his pace.

"What's happened?" he demanded, when, because there was nothing else she could do, she let him in. "You're supposed to be having dinner with me. Remember?"

"Yes," said Sarah. "I'm sorry, I——"

Brett's eyes fell on the sensible suit. "But not in that," he added authoritatively. "I will not sit down to eat opposite a beautiful woman who insists on disguising herself as a neat but elderly potato. Take it off."

"I will not——" began Sarah.

"Yes, you will. Go on, now." He gave her a little shove toward the bedroom.

"Don't be ridiculous."

"I'm not being ridiculous, but I *am* getting impatient." When Sarah didn't move, he added silkily, "If that tailored abomination isn't off in twenty seconds I'm going to take it off for you."

Sarah gasped, and gazed up incredulously. He was smiling, but it was a very determined smile and there was a distinctly implacable glint in his tawny eyes.

"I mean it," he said softly.

Sarah had no doubt he did. She gave him a venomous look, put her chin in the air—and fled.

When she emerged from the bedroom again, now dressed in a neat gray number with a very slight dip at the neck, Brett was leaning against the wall in the hallway with his arms crossed, looking like an imperious Roman senator waiting to chastise a tardy slave.

Sarah, already annoyed at his high-handedness, felt a ripple of resentment, but decided there was nothing to be gained by showing it. She didn't intend to play the role of slave for long anyway, but just now the senator seemed to have the upper hand.

He ran his eyes quickly over the neat gray number, then rolled them up at the ceiling. "All right. It's better than the suit, anyway," he said resignedly. "Come on."

He waited impatiently while she pulled a light raincoat from the cupboard, then grabbed her arm and hurried her through the door.

The rain was pelting down now, so they ran the short distance between their houses and arrived, breathless and very wet, on his front porch.

"You're soaked," murmured Sarah, as he put his hand on the doorknob. Without knowing she was going to do it she reached up and touched her fingers to the wet fabric clinging to his chest. All his clothes were clinging and she could see the damp sinews of his body outlined all the way down from his chest to his well-formed calves.

Brett glanced at her hand, smiled enigmatically, and covered it tightly with his own.

Sarah swallowed and tried to pull away. Their eyes met, something hot snaked between them and she knew without a doubt that she was playing with a fire that could easily turn into an inferno. But when he released her and pushed her ahead of him through the door she didn't even try to resist.

As soon as they were inside their noses were assailed by the smell of frying chicken, and the pulsating tension that had been between them faded.

"It smells as though it's done," said Brett, dripping his way across the hall into the kitchen. Sarah removed her wet coat and followed him.

Oh, it's done all right, she thought gloomily. Overcooked chicken, it is! As Brett pulled a tray of dried-out french fries from the oven she noted that her second prediction had come true also. Two out of three. Not bad. Now all they needed was soggy salad and she'd have run up a perfect score.

"You go and get changed," she said to him, "and could you hang up my coat while you're at it? I'll see to this. What else is there?"

"Coleslaw. I bought it at the deli yesterday."

"Jackpot," she muttered, handing him her coat and moving across to the stove.

"Hmm?" Brett looked puzzled.

"Nothing. Go and take those wet things off."

"And if I don't, will you threaten to take them off for me?" he asked hopefully.

"No, I'll leave that kind of domineering sexism to you. If you want to catch pneumonia, be my guest."

Brett grinned. "You're my guest, I believe, but if you want to make yourself useful you can set the table. The knives and forks are in that drawer and we might as well eat in the kitchen. Fried chicken and deli coleslaw don't merit the gourmet treatment."

Sarah couldn't have agreed more. "Are you going to get changed?" she asked. "Or am I to have the pleasure of watching you eat with that wet shirt plastered to your skin?''

''Would it be a pleasure?'' he asked, tawny eyes teasing her.

''No.'' Sarah turned away and began to examine the overcooked contents of the oven. That way he might think the color in her cheeks was caused by external heat only.

Brett smiled and loped nonchalantly out of the room. Sarah's eyes followed him. That broad back, those tight thighs and the way his wet trousers stretched across his hips... Mmm.

No, you don't, Sarah. Never mind. She brought herself up short. Fried chicken, that was what she was supposed to be thinking. *Dry* fried chicken at that.

Fifteen minutes later the two of them sat down to Brett's idea of suitable company fare, and as the table was small and their knees kept touching underneath it Sarah was very glad that he was now wearing a decently bulky black sweater over a well-worn pair of denim jeans.

They ate quickly, much to Sarah's relief as there didn't seem much to linger over, talked briefly about Tony, the weather, the horrors of moving and other such innocuous subjects, and as soon as they were finished Brett told her to leave everything to him and make herself at home in the living room.

It was a large room, but it didn't seem large, mainly because numerous packing crates were still piled up around the walls and a collection of oddly assorted chairs was strewn untidily under the window. But there was an old, rust-colored pull-out couch that looked comfortable. A red maple coffee table stood in front of it and Sarah presumed it was the start of Brett's attempt to arrange the room. If he was making an attempt, which seemed doubtful.

She sat down on the couch and reached idly for a veterinary trade magazine which was lying on top of a pile of books—mostly about exotic animals and presumably belonging to Tony. But she could hear Brett clattering in the kitchen and her mind wouldn't stay on the technical aspects of the latest abdominal surgery for cats. Instead it kept returning to the man in the other room and her own confused feelings about him—and she remembered the flame that had flared between them when she put her hand on the wet shirt clinging to his chest.

She was frightened, there was no getting away from it, frightened of Brett who had given her no tangible cause for fear beyond mocking her a little, losing his temper on occasion, and once, deliberately but not savagely, kissing her on the lips.

So what was she scared of? It was true that there was a kind of controlled violence about him sometimes that seemed to simmer just below the surface—but it wasn't only that. She turned a page of the magazine without seeing what was on it—and she knew the answer. She was afraid of the physical excitement she felt in his presence, afraid of the power he had over emotions that had been safely locked away for so many years—and at this precise moment she was frightened because he was coming into the room carrying two steaming cups of coffee and she knew he was going to make straight for the empty space beside her.

He put the coffee down, splashing a little on to the red maple table, and without waiting for an invitation lowered himself down next to her. When he stretched an arm along the back and she felt his fingers touch her hair, she jumped and started away from him.

Brett's smile was hypnotic. Dangerous. "What's the matter?" he asked softly, turning to face her. "I thought we'd established that I don't bite unless I'm invited."

With a tremendous effort, Sarah returned his smile without betraying the turmoil that was raging inside her. "Of course you don't," she said brightly. "I just don't like being touched."

A stillness came over Brett's face then, a stillness in which his eyes glittered at her, bright and cutting as a razor—and in those eyes Sarah thought she saw a deep, abiding bitterness that was strangely at odds with her perception of him as a self-confident, physical, not very complex man.

"I didn't mean to offend you," she murmured, feeling she had to say something to wipe that look of—surely it wasn't suffering?—from his face.

"Why not?" he asked unpleasantly. "Does it matter?"

"I—yes, it does."

"You surprise me. Very well, then, you haven't offended me."

"Oh," she said doubtfully. "Then I hope——"

He didn't let her finish. "You haven't offended me because you're not telling the truth, are you?" His fingers curved around her neck. "I've had plenty of experience with women who don't like to be touched and I don't think you're one of them. Underneath all that touch-me-not armor there's a passionate woman waiting to come to life. Isn't there? So why are you playing games with me, Sarah?" His eyes were hard, demanding, impossible to avoid.

"I'm not," she cried, reacting angrily to his harshness. "What makes you think you have only to snap your fingers, Brett Jackson, to have any woman you fancy swooning all over you? Hasn't it ever occurred to you that there may be at least one woman in this world who isn't interested in falling into your arms?"

The eyes were two topaz slits now, so hard she could almost feel them cut. "Yes. It has. As I told you, my experience in that line is considerable. Believe it or not. But I had the mistaken impression that you were different, that beneath all that frozen hard glitter there might be genuine gold. Apparently I was wrong. I apologize.''

Sarah gaped at him. "Apologize?" she whispered. "For calling me genuine gold?"

"No. For calling you passionate. You seem to feel it's an insult.''

She closed her eyes because she couldn't bear the scorn she read in his. After what seemed a very long, silent interval she opened them again and saw that Brett was watching her with a look that was no longer scornful or angry but in some surprising way—just sad. And she thought with a sudden flash of insight: he's not only an arrogant, uncomplicated, lustful man on the make. He's been hurt too.

Those lines she hadn't noticed before, the deep ones around his eyes, they hadn't been put there by some careless accident of nature. They had grown there, probably over a long period of time, and for some reason her violent reaction to his touch had opened up an ancient wound. She didn't understand how, but she knew she had hurt much more than his male ego.

"I'm sorry," she said slowly. "I was wrong. You're not just an arrogant stud, are you, Brett? I shouldn't have said that.''

"You didn't. Not in so many words. But I gather you meant it.''

"I suppose I did. I don't any more. You've been hurt too, haven't you?''

He dismissed that with an abrupt flick of his hand, and she noticed how the wide leather strap of his watchband seemed to emphasize the strength of his forearms.

"Haven't we all? I'll survive. What about you, Sarah?"

"Me?"

"Why do you take such pains to play the Snow Queen?"

He was asking her point-blank why she wouldn't let him get close to her, why she wouldn't let any man get close. But because he had touched some chord, some need, deep within her, for the first time since the disaster of Jason, she felt that she might be able to tell someone what had happened. Someone who wasn't one of her parents who already knew. Someone who was Brett Jackson, her next-door neighbor.

She took a long breath, and unwittingly her hand brushed against the black wool covering his arm. Brett saw her startled jump as she pulled her fingers away, and he smiled bleakly. Then, very deliberately, he picked up the hand and held it against his chest.

"There," he said softly. "That wasn't so bad, was it?"

No, it wasn't bad. It was nice. She liked the rough feel of the wool on her skin and she liked the knowledge that his hard chest lay just beneath the tips of her fingers.

She shook her head wordlessly.

"Want to talk, Snow Queen?"

It wasn't a gibe meant to mock her. It was his way of saying that he wanted to understand, might even help her if he could. At least, looking into those molten eyes of his, it seemed that way.

At that moment nothing could have stopped her talking.

"I wasn't always a—a Snow Queen, Brett," she said, in a voice so low he had to strain to hear her. "You see— when I was seventeen I was going to be married." She hesitated, then forced herself to go on. "To a man I was very much in love with..."

"Don't stop," he pressed her.

Sarah moistened her lips. "Then—then just four days before the wedding he—he—my fiancé, Jason—he left town." Her voice broke. "Without even saying goodbye."

# CHAPTER SIX

BRETT'S fist tightened around Sarah's hand as he laid it lightly on his thigh and linked his fingers with hers.

"The bastard," he said very softly. "The rotten bastard."

Sarah nodded. "Yes. Only I didn't realize that until too late."

"What happened?" He was insistent, not allowing her to evade the question.

She blew her nose, moistened her lips and stared fixedly at the patterned rug in front of the fireplace. "I—he was my boss. Before Angela. There wasn't a law office in town till he came, and everyone thought it was kind of unusual that a young man would want to set up on his own in a quiet little place like Caley Cove. But it turned out he was just marking time. He had connections, and when the big opportunity in Washington came along—he took it."

"Abandoning the bride he was supposed to marry in just four days' time? Are you telling me the truth? That doesn't make sense, Sarah." Brett stared at the back of her head, his brows drawn together, not able to accept what she was telling him.

"Oh, yes, it did," said Sarah bitterly. "He knew the move was coming up. He just didn't tell me. I was a— a physical convenience in the meantime. Until he was ready to move on. He left a letter. That was more convenient than talking to me, you see. Less awkward."

"I don't understand."

"Neither did I at the time. I thought he loved me. But his letter explained that, although he was fond of me, I was just a small-town girl who wouldn't fit in in Washington—wouldn't help further his career."

"Then why in *hell* did he get involved with you in the first place?" The fingers of Brett's free hand clenched tightly on her shoulder and the fierceness in his voice made Sarah glance up, startled.

"That's easy," she answered him, her brown eyes very wide and clear. "He was a—a lusty sort of man. His bodily appetites were quite—healthy——"

"You mean he was oversexed, as well as a bastard."

"Yes. I suppose he was, looking back on it. And there weren't many available women in Caley Cove. Most of them leave as soon as they finish school. But I was very available, very obviously moonstruck—and right there for the plucking. In his office."

"That I can understand and even sympathize with. Even at seventeen you must have been... Well, never mind. But what I don't accept is that it was necessary to promise you marriage when he didn't intend to go through with it."

Sarah shrugged and looked away. "It wasn't necessary as far as I was concerned. I was totally besotted. But my parents said I was too young to be going out with a thirty-year-old man. They wouldn't let me see him outside office hours and they started insisting I look for another job. So he asked me to marry him to prove his intentions were honorable—and after that Mother and Dad couldn't say much. We were engaged, but, because they were still deeply suspicious, he pretended he was anxious to set a date." She smiled wanly. "I don't think he expected to be taken up on it. He thought my parents would want us to wait. But they didn't. They were afraid

I'd end up in his bed if we had to wait, and of course we didn't tell them that we'd crossed that bridge already.''

"No, I don't imagine you would," said Brett shortly. He scowled, and ran his eyes briefly over her drooping figure.

Hearing the harsh rasp of his voice, Sarah looked up doubtfully and saw that his lips had compressed into a bleak line. His eyes had darkened too and she knew he was angry. She didn't think the anger was directed at her, and yet he seemed to be holding something in, some violent urge to beat something or someone to a bloody pulp.

"What is it?" she asked shakily. "Have I said something?"

"You've said plenty."

"Oh—then perhaps..." She started to get up, but Brett grabbed her wrist and pulled her back down beside him.

"Perhaps you should tell me the rest of it," he said, not gently, but making an obvious effort to keep whatever demon was tormenting him in check.

"Very well," she replied tonelessly, taking a long breath. "We did set a date. And I bought a dress and sent out all the invitations. And Jason went on using me. Only I didn't know he was using me, of course. I thought he was loving me." Her voice cracked. "He never intended to marry me, I'm sure, but he thought he might as well get all the pleasure he could out of the situation until it was time for him to go. I found out later that the call from Washington came two weeks before we were supposed to be married, so he just got his affairs in order, arranged the move—and when the time came he left. No fuss, no embarrassing scenes. Exactly as he wanted.''

Brett's face was unreadable. "And you'd no idea? Sarah, I know you were young, but surely you weren't stupid? There must have been signs..."

"I was *very* stupid. But there weren't many signs. He did suddenly insist on hotel rooms instead of his house, but he said that was because he wanted to surprise me when we were married. I thought he was redecorating for me. All I was worried about was that he might have picked colors I didn't like." She laughed and, hearing that laugh, Brett lifted his fist and smashed it down on his knee.

"Your parents," he growled. "Didn't they real-ize——?"

"They weren't happy, but they felt that if Jason was the man I wanted...and no, of course they never thought he'd just run off. We're not used to that sort of ruth-lessness in Caley Cove. We have plenty of scandals, Lord knows—I was one of them—but usually they're caused by ignorance or hormones or something—not by delib-erate, calculated self-interest."

Brett closed his eyes and muttered an oath. Quite gently, he put his fingers beneath her chin and forced her to look at him. "Is that why——?" he began.

"Yes, that's why," she interrupted quickly. "But I'm over it now."

"Are you?" he asked. His eyes wouldn't let her look away.

"I—well, yes. Of course." In a strange way, it was true.

Perhaps she hadn't been over the hurt after all until this moment. But now, with Brett's hard gaze still on her, implacable and at the same time almost tender, she felt light, as if a great burden had been lifted. Surprise, too, that at last she had been able to talk about the past without wanting to run away and hide from the world's curiosity and pity. Or from Brett's. Only he wasn't expressing much pity, was he? Instead he was looking at her with a stern demand, and all at once she felt vulnerable, soft—capable again of being hurt. And she didn't like it.

"If you're over it, why do you live the life of a hermit, Sarah?" Brett wasn't about to let her off the hook. "Why are you afraid to let anyone near you?"

"I don't live the life of a hermit," she said quickly, unbearably conscious of his fingers against her skin. "I go out sometimes."

"With men?"

"No, by myself or with Angela, and my parents—and schoolfriends sometimes when they come home for visits. I like it this way. I'm happy here, very comfortable."

Sarah's voice had an edge of desperation to it, as if she was trying to convince herself as much as him.

"Then why are you afraid to let me touch you?" he asked softly. "I know you don't find me wholly repulsive."

"No, of course I don't." She gulped and pushed herself back against the arm of the couch, leaving a yawning gap between them. "I don't want any involvement, that's all. And besides, you were touching me just now. I didn't stop you."

"No, you forgot yourself for a moment, didn't you? What if I tried to touch you now, Sarah?"

For one mad, irrelevant moment she wondered if he had looked at his wife like that. All warm and glinting and—predatory. His wife who had, just possibly, taken her own life. "I—don't—my coffee's getting cold," she gasped.

"You see? You're running away again," he said softly. "You can't hide from life forever, you know, my dear."

"I'm not hiding from life. I told you. I'm quite happy the way I am."

"Are you? Perhaps. But you're missing more than you know. I'd like to kiss you again, Sarah."

"No. You can't..." Her fingers scrabbled frantically behind her as she tried to lever herself further away. But Brett only moved relentlessly along the seat toward her and in a moment his hands were on her shoulders and he was looking straight into her eyes.

"One kiss won't lead to that involvement you're so scared of," he assured her. "You might even find you enjoy it."

His left hand moved to the back of her head, tangling in her short hair. His right hand lifted her chin up. The gold flecks in his eyes were like chips of fire, glowing and hypnotic, and his knees brushed against hers as she started away. She gasped, and slowly the knees parted, sliding firmly and intimately up the diaphanous nylon covering her legs until she was trapped between his thighs, paralyzed, almost unable to breathe.

As she gazed at him, trying to conquer the delicious and long forgotten sensations spiraling throughout her body, his hand slid down her back and he bent toward her so that she was half lying against the rust-colored arm. And his fingers played a subtle music on her spine. Then somehow she was stretched out on the couch. Brett's firm, tough body was leaning over her—and his lips were moving very close. As she watched him, not able to move, her own lips parted in willing invitation. Then she gave a soft, wordless cry and wound her arms around his neck, and in that moment his mouth came down over hers, as for the second time in her life she knew what it felt like to be kissed by a man who she could almost believe was not thinking only of himself.

It was a long kiss, gentle at first, then more passionate, and for one wild instant Sarah thought, yes. Yes, this is right. *Brett's* right, this is what life's meant to be. But as her fingers caught in his thick, waving hair and her body began to strain up toward him, suddenly, unbelievably, she became aware of a sort of shuffling sound whispering from the other end of the room.

Sarah froze, and Brett paused and lifted his head. She saw him twist his neck to look over his shoulder, and then he muttered, "Blasted bloody mutts," raised himself on his arms and sat up.

"What is it?" She gaped at him, her heart fluttering annoyingly as a surprising sense of loss crept into her limbs.

"Dogs," he said briefly, pushing himself to his feet and straightening the bulky black sweater which seemed to add even more breadth to his already impressive frame.

"Dogs?" she repeated blankly.

"Sparky and Pickles. They don't like being left out in the rain."

"But I thought they lived outside."

"Not all the time. And the catch on the back door doesn't work too well. I forgot to lock it when I went to get you, and if I'm not mistaken those two muddy miscreants are on their way upstairs to take up residence on Tony's bed."

"Oh," said Sarah, not troubling to point out that he had read her the riot act for leaving her door open. She could see from the way his eyes slanted away from her that he was remembering that occasion all too well.

He cleared his throat. "Back in a minute. I'll settle them in the kitchen."

Sarah realized she was still stretched out on the couch. She sat up hastily and pulled her gray skirt down around her knees as the sounds of scuffling and panting and paws pattering on wood drifted down from upstairs— along with Brett's voice yelling something about miserable mobile mudpies who knew damn well they weren't supposed to be on beds.

There was more scuffling, then the noise of two dogs erupting into the kitchen. A moment later two furry bodies hurtled through the door and began to rush gleefully at Sarah.

"Stay!" roared Brett. "Out. Both of you."

The dogs slid to a halt, ears flying, looked reproachfully over their shoulders at their master and then, somewhat to Sarah's surprise, they trotted obediently back to the kitchen.

"Aren't they allowed in here?" she asked curiously. Brett didn't *seem* the house-proud type, but perhaps she'd misread him...

"Not when they're covered in mud," he said shortly. "They've been gallivanting in the flowerbeds—again."

"Oh," said Sarah doubtfully, stealing a cautious glance at his indignant, glowering face.

He intercepted the glance, held her gaze for a moment, and then quite suddenly his teeth parted in a broad, self-mocking grin. "So much for Brett Jackson the disciplinarian," he said cheerfully. "The day we got those two rejects I told Tony they were not to sleep on his bed. Under any circumstances. And to be fair, I never *catch* them there. But it's an extraordinary thing—every time I feel his bedspread in the morning there are two dog-sized warm spots on the end."

Sarah laughed. "You don't really care, do you?" she remarked with sudden perception. "I have a feeling that if you did there wouldn't be any warm spots."

Brett shook his head. "Found out again," he said ruefully. "You're right. There wouldn't."

His eyes were traveling over her so warmly that Sarah felt startlingly self-conscious. She glanced at her watch, stood up and said quickly, "I'd better go now. It's getting late."

"Nonsense. It's the weekend. And we have some unfinished business to see to."

"No, said Sarah. "No, we haven't. Really..."

"What's the matter, Sarah? Running away still? I'm not Bluebeard, you know. Or Jason. I promise you won't come to any harm."

"No, of course I won't. It's just..."

"Just what?"

"Well, I—I..." She had been on the point of saying, "I don't honestly know," when it came to her, quite devastatingly, that she did know.

Brett was a very attractive, very persuasive man, and it would be all too easy to fall in love with his good looks and casual, contagious charm. But she'd been that route before, and it had been the biggest mistake of her life. Apart from that, there was another little matter to contend with. The matter of Tony's "Aunt Elise," It looked very much as if Brett was attempting to have his cake and eat it as well. He *said* Elise was just an old friend now, but he had shot off like a bullet when she'd asked him to help her move. And the other day her mother had mentioned that Molly had mentioned seeing him with a tall, blond woman. She had refused to pay much attention at the time, determined that it wouldn't become her business. But now... Could there really be smoke without fire?

No. Ice maiden she had been for the past ten years, and ice maiden she would remain. Or Snow Queen, as Brett had called her. Snow was safe. Soft, secure, no sharp edges—no painful passion.

"It's just that I want to go home now," she said firmly, avoiding the warm, seductive gleam in his eyes and pulling her wide mouth into a severely businesslike line. "Will you fetch my coat, please."

The seductive gleam faded and once more the golden eyes turned opaque. "I see," he said enigmatically. "So you believe . . . I suppose I might have known. All right, I'll fetch your coat, then, if that's what you want." His voice had turned cold now, and his fists were clenched hard against his thighs.

"Yes—yes, it is." She wished she didn't sound breathless and that her heart would stop jumping around in her chest. And what might he have known?

The muscles of his mouth tightened and he gave a slight shrug before he turned away. "I left your coat in the hall cupboard," he said, in a flat, uninterested voice.

"Yes," she muttered, feeling like a fool as she watched him swing unhurriedly out of the room. In her attempt to seem calm, cool and in complete control of the situation, she had sent him off to collect a coat she was entirely capable of fetching for herself. It wasn't as if this were some grand social occasion, yet here she was, waiting for service like the helpless star of an old and very bad movie. She hesitated, and then followed him into the hall.

"Is it still raining?" she asked brightly, trying to sound relaxed and casual.

"Ah. The weather." He raised one dark, derisive eyebrow in that way that she had always thought physically out of the question.

"I said, is it still raining?" she repeated, puzzled.

"I know you did. The weather. A nice *safe* topic."

Sarah eyed him balefully. "Oh, never mind," she snapped, reaching for the coat and starting to put it on. "I'll find out soon enough, won't I?"

"I expect you will," he replied without noticeable interest. Then, efficiently, and not allowing his fingers to linger on her for one second longer than was necessary, he held out her sleeve and eased the still damp raincoat over her shoulders.

She fastened the belt and stepped past him to open the door. But his hand was on the knob before she could reach it, and for a moment he just stood there, a surprisingly menacing figure, staring down at her with a hard, unreadable look on his handsome face. Eventually, after prolonging the moment uncomfortably, he moved deliberately aside to let her pass.

"Thank you for the supper," she said, not looking at him. "It was very kind of you to have me."

"Wasn't it?" he agreed from behind her.

She was halfway down the path now, and, realizing he was still with her, she looked up with quick suspicion. "There's no need to come with me," she assured him. "I can certainly make it back to my own front door."

"I'm sure you can. Nevertheless, it's dark. I'll see you home."

"It's still raining. You'll get wet."

"I don't disintegrate in the rain, Sarah."

No, she thought frustratedly. You certainly don't. You just get sexier. She turned her head firmly to the front so that she wouldn't see the raindrops shining in his hair or the way his jeans clung damply to his thighs.

As soon as they reached her bungalow she pulled out a key and started to fumble with the lock.

"I'm all right now. You can go home," she said quickly.

He waited until she had the door open and had stepped across the threshold before replying evenly, "I intend to. Good night, Sarah."

"Good night." She glanced up then, acutely conscious that she was losing something—no, *rejecting* something that she might very well find out later she wanted to keep.

But it was too late. His eyes flicked coolly over her wet hair and dripping raincoat, and then smiled, a tight, almost chilling smile, said good-night again, and strode away down the path.

"Damn," said Sarah out loud as she slammed the door shut behind her. "Damn, damn, damn, damn, damn."

She pulled off her coat and threw it with uncharacteristic carelessness at the cupboard, and it occurred to her that her words—well, word—had a familiar ring to it. Wasn't there some play in which the hero kept saying "damn" when it finally dawned on him that he'd grown accustomed to the heroine's face?

She stamped into the kitchen to put the kettle on. Yes, there was. So did that mean she had grown accustomed to Brett's face? It was the sort of face one could very easily acquire a taste for. And he had been sympathetic, if a little intimidating, about Jason. In fact until she'd remembered Elise she had felt that he might actually be a man she could trust, a man who wouldn't use her and let her down. Only Elise was no phantom. Molly was a gossip, but not a deliberate liar. Sarah sighed, and wiped a nonexistent grease spot off the stove. Of course, there *could* be a perfectly ordinary explanation. Couldn't there? She shook her head. There could be, but it was much more likely that Brett was the same as all the rest: out for what he could get. She had been right not to let her guard down after all, to rebuild the protective wall of ice which she had, very briefly, allowed to melt.

He had seemed so—so hurt, though. Not just angry, but bitter, as if he too had suffered. Of course he *had* lost his wife, but if her mother's grapevine was correct that hadn't been the tragedy of his life.

Sarah shrugged irritably and pulled the whistling kettle off the stove. Obviously she had misinterpreted his reaction, because surely the only thing she had hurt was his pride?

All the same, there had been a moment when she'd trusted him. Wasn't it possible that she was wrong? Possible that she could take his sympathy and interest at face value?

"You're a fool, Sarah Malone," she said loudly. "And you ought to know better. Brett Jackson is sincere all right. He sincerely wants to get you into his bed."

So? muttered another traitorous voice in her head. What's bad about that?

"So I've been there," she shouted, banging her cup down on the table and splashing coffee all over the floor. "I've been there, and I am not, repeat *not*, going to let some man take advantage of me again. For a few hours of dubious pleasure? It's not worth it."

She gave a short groan of exasperation and went to get a cloth to wipe the floor.

Sarah rubbed her eyes sleepily. What time was it? And what was that noise outside her door? Ten o'clock. And that wasn't a noise, that was an earthshaking unholy cacophony. Not just fists pounding on wood, but a man's voice raised in some sort of raucous, tuneless warbling that she was all too well aware she had heard before. Only last time it had been accompanied by hammer blows descending with relentless precision on two dog kennels.

She mouthed a word of which she knew her mother would not approve, jumped out of bed, pulled on her blue robe and stormed out into the hall.

"Don't you know it's Sunday morning?" she yelled, as she swung the door open. "What the hell do you think you're doing, Brett Jackson?"

The warbling stopped at once as Brett, clad in jeans and the black sweater again, moved her carefully out of his way, stepped in and closed the door behind him.

"Serenading you," he said calmly. "It was the only way I could think of to make you open this door."

# CHAPTER SEVEN

SARAH glared at Brett. "That," she said furiously, "was not serenading. That was caterwauling."

Brett shrugged. "I tried," he said ruefully. "And it did get you out of bed."

"I thought you wanted to get me into bed," she said without thinking—and immediately blushed a healthy fire-engine red.

"I do," he replied with devastating honesty. "But I've decided to postpone that pleasure for a while. Red suits you, by the way. You should blush more often."

"Oh," exclaimed Sarah, her color fading rapidly as indignation overcame embarrassment. "Oh! Really you are the most obnoxious, arrogant, egotistical——" She stopped abruptly. "What do you mean, you've decided to postpone the pleasure?"

"I mean that if I set my mind to it I don't think I'd have any trouble at all persuading you into my bed. The only problem is, I don't think you'd ever forgive me. Not at this stage."

Sarah swallowed. "Would that matter?"

"Mmm." His mouth twisted in a wry, regretful grimace. "I'm afraid it would."

"Why?" she demanded, placing her hands aggressively on her hips and forgetting all about keeping her robe closed. "You'd have got what you wanted, wouldn't you?"

He shook his head and moved away from her to rest his shoulders against the wall. "Possibly. I haven't made up my mind about that." His amber eyes gleamed at her, a little malevolently. "I scared you away on Friday, Sarah, and that was stupid of me. I know you've been hurt." He stared stonily at a spot above her head. "Haven't we all. But I should have taken things slowly, waited until you felt comfortable, I suppose, instead of getting angry when you held me off. I'm sorry."

He didn't sound sorry. The sensuous curve of his mouth straightened as he spoke, and Sarah wondered if his apology was made with an ulterior motive. Again she had a feeling that there was some shadow in his past that was not as simple as losing a wife he loved—or didn't love?

"You're quite lovely, you know," he was going on, in that deep velvet voice she loved to hear. "Even in those unfeminine clothes you usually wear. I'm afraid my obnoxious, arrogant, egotistical male libido took over any gentlemanly instincts I might have had. I wanted so much to kiss you that I did." His eyes narrowed suddenly. "And you enjoyed it as much as I did, didn't you? Until you dredged up a good reason to hold me off."

She gaped at him, stunned that in a few short moments he could proffer a reluctant apology, practically seduce her with his voice, and then, in a matter of seconds, turn into a sneering accuser. As she stared up at him, abruptly he turned his back. When he turned around again the narrow-eyed look had faded.

"This is futile, isn't it?" he said evenly. "So how about we start again from the beginning?" He spoke with an arrogant confidence that annoyed Sarah almost as much as it charmed her.

"I—I..." Unwillingly her eyes took in the muscular length of his body lounging against her wall as if he belonged there, and the beginnings of an oh, so seductive smile. And his eyes, hooded now as he waited for her answer. Oh, Lord, she couldn't say no to this man. "I—I guess we can," she whispered. "Yes, of course we can." She took a deep breath. "And I'm sorry too—if I misled you."

His hands dropped to his sides. "All right, Miss Havisham." He eased himself away from the wall and moved toward her. "It's a truce. I'll forgive you if you'll forgive me. Provided you'll come out with me today."

"Out?" said Sarah, squeaking like a startled mouse.

"Mmm. You know as in out on a date. I thought we might drive to Lake Crescent."

"But—the rain . . ."

"It's stopped. Our Indian summer is back. Hadn't you noticed?"

Sarah laughed for the first time that morning. "No, I hadn't. You pushed your way into my house without giving me a chance to check the weather. And I don't know if it's escaped your attention, but there aren't any windows in this hall."

"So there aren't."

"Why did you call me Miss Havisham?"

"Dickens. *Great Expectations*."

"Oh," said Sarah slowly. "You mean the old lady who was jilted on her wedding day. And stopped all the clocks and never took off her wedding gown again."

"That's the one."

"But—I'm not like that. I haven't stopped the clocks, and I gave my dress away—oh, years ago."

"Yes, and you traded it in for severe brown tweeds and your navy blue armor, didn't you? Sometimes I think there's not much difference between you and that grim old lady."

She frowned. "Of course there is. Don't be ridiculous . . ."

"All right, then prove it to me. Come out with me today, Sarah Havisham."

As he spoke he lifted his hands to drop them over her shoulders, and Sarah, looking up into commanding gold-flecked eyes, heard herself answer, "Yes. Yes, all right. I'll come."

"Good. In that case I'll go home to feed the dogs and Fawcett, which will give you time to get ready. I'll be back to get you in an hour."

Sarah nodded dumbly as Brett patted her casually on the head—just as if I'm one of his dogs, she thought resentfully—and with a hearty slam of the door he was gone.

She stared blankly at the still shuddering panels. When she found she was still staring five minutes later, she gave herself a mental shake and padded into the kitchen to make her breakfast.

Now what had she got herself into? On Friday she had decided that Brett Jackson could not have any part in her life, and here she was just two days later, agreeing to go out with him for the day. It didn't make sense.

But whether it made sense or not, precisely one hour later she was dressed in jeans—the oldest and most faded pair she owned, which she was aware were still tiresomely well-fitting—and a baggy white sweater on top of a navy blue blouse. If Brett thought he could dictate the colors she wore, he would find out very quickly he was mistaken.

She was just pulling her denim jacket out of the cupboard when Brett's loud rap sounded on the door.

"Better," he murmured cryptically, as he sized up her jeans and sweater with practiced speed. "Much better."

"What's better?" asked Sarah, knowing quite well, and not sure whether she was pleased or annoyed.

"The jeans. I always suspected you had a figure underneath all those tweedy skirts. And you have. A very nice one, if I may say so." Quite casually, he took her arm, turned her around and, as they made their way outside, gave her a possessive little pat on the bottom.

"You may not say so," she said crossly. "And in any case you can keep your hands off my figure and stop patting me as if I were a dog."

Brett gave an exaggerated sigh and waved her into the station wagon which was parked at the edge of the road. "I'll try," he promised. "But it isn't going to be easy. Oh, and by the way, that wasn't anything like the way I pat a dog."

Sarah turned to glare at him as he swung his long legs up beside her, but he was grinning with such wicked amusement that she changed her mind and laughed instead.

She was still laughing an hour later when the station wagon pulled up beside a rambling log-cabin-style hotel beside the lake.

"You're beautiful when you laugh," said Brett softly. "Did you know that?"

Sarah shook her head, and sobered instantly to say with a trace of irritation, and even a little fear, "No, I'm not. And I don't even know why I was laughing."

"Yes, you are. And you were laughing because you're enjoying my company for a change—whether you want to admit it or not."

It was true, of course. But somehow, just for an instant, she had felt a trace of alarm as the car came to a halt beside the hotel. Years ago, ten years to be exact, she had stopped at a place very like this one with Jason. And they had remained for a lot more than lunch...

She stared at Brett now, saw the golden lights dancing in his eyes and replied sheepishly, almost on a note of relief, "You know, I do believe you're right."

"I know I'm right," he said, easing his body out of the car and strolling around to open her door. "Because I'm enjoying your company too, Sarah Malone." He took her hand. "Are you starving?"

His eyes caressed her, and for a moment Sarah was conscious that it wasn't food she was starved for at all. Oh, no. What she felt at this moment was a hunger that had nothing whatever to do with the fact that she hadn't had lunch. Then common sense, and an empty feeling in her stomach, forced her to consider more immediate matters. "Yes," she admitted, smiling at him. "I am hungry. Let's eat."

Hand in hand they strolled into the warm, carpeted lobby of the hotel and from there into a high-ceilinged, brightly lit dining room where they were shown to a table for two by the window.

"It's lovely," said Sarah, looking out over the sparkling beauty of the lake to the wooded slopes reflected in the gray-blue waters.

"Yes," said Brett, his eyes on her face, warm and approving. "It is, isn't it?"

Sarah turned away, unaccountably embarrassed. Funny, she had felt so comfortable with Brett in the car, comfortable and happy in a way she had never been with Jason. And yet they had not spoken of anything that mattered. Instead they had exclaimed at the thistle seeds drifting in white puffs across the road, and at the ducks energetically pursuing their lunch in the lake. Then they had chuckled over the antics of Pickles and Sparky, and Sarah had waxed enthusiastic about the intricacies of model boat building. When Brett said modeling was an unusual hobby for a woman, she had tossed her head and asked him if he would prefer it if she crocheted—or painted flowers.

"No," he had replied immediately. "I'd prefer it if you were like my mother, who enjoys cooking so much that she always has mountains of food left over for needy neighbors." He slanted his eyes at her with teasing but, she suspected, not altogether flippant insinuation.

Thinking about that moment now, as a motherly looking waitress took their orders, Sarah grinned.

"I told you you ought to do that more often," Brett told her. "You have the most enchanting smile of any woman I've known."

"What's this?" she asked suspiciously. "Act Two in *The Seduction of Sarah Malone*? It isn't going to work, you know, Brett Jackson."

He groaned and shook his head. "Don't you even know how to accept a compliment, woman? I've already told you I have no intention of seducing you before you're ready."

The chicken salad came just then and it was a minute or two before Sarah was able to answer. "I'm not going to be ready," she informed him flatly. "Not ever."

"Why not?" His voice was soft but demanding, his eyes disconcertingly stern. But when she said nothing he went on more gently, "You're still afraid I'll hurt you, aren't you, Sarah? Why won't you trust me?"

Sarah dropped a slice of tomato off her fork and glued her eyes on her plate. "Because—because I'm afraid to, I guess. Jason told me I could trust him too. But I couldn't. And now you say I can trust you, but you're still seeing Elise. At least—Molly Bracken said she saw you with a woman in a restaurant and——"

"I am *not* Jason. And I am not seeing Elise." Brett's lionlike roar caused several heads to turn in their direction. "How often do I have to tell you that, Sarah?"

With an effort, he lowered his voice a few octaves and the spectators looked reluctantly away. "Yes, a long time ago Elise and I were—close to each other. She supported me through some very bad times, and for a while we *were* more than friends. But in the end we decided what was happening just wasn't right for either of us, and we parted—very amicably. I helped her move, and yes, I did run into her the other day. We had coffee together. So what? Oh, and while we're on the subject, after Elise there was a woman called Mary-Jo. And that, my dear, I assure you, is all there is to it. Elise is a friend, Mary-Jo is history now too, and if I hear one more word about either of those two ladies it will give me great pleasure to tan your beautiful hide."

As she gaped at him, not sure whether to laugh, slap him or apologize, he grimaced, and brushed a hand over his eyes. "Don't worry, I'm not really a combination of Bluebeard, Svengali and Jack the Ripper in one," he assured her wryly.

"Well—not Jack the Ripper," murmured Sarah, as a very small smile began to pull at the edge of her mouth.

"I'm relieved to hear it. It's a beginning anyway." Brett pushed his plate away and leaned back in his chair to gaze pensively at the high white ceiling.

"You're telling me the truth, aren't you?" she said with sudden perception as her eyes fastened on the muscles in his neck.

"Mmm. It's a habit of mine." He lowered his eyes and gave her a softly sardonic smile. "Now eat your chicken like a good girl, stop looking for problems that don't exist, and when you've finished we'll go for a nice walk in the woods together—and I assure you that, although I may find it a strain, I won't make the slightest attempt to rape you. Is it a deal?" He lifted his eyebrows inquiringly.

Sarah sighed. He was patronizing her again, but it was only a teasing patronage. She took several mouthfuls of chicken and gradually the comfort and security she had felt earlier began to overcome her doubt and suspicion.

"All right," she agreed. "It's a deal."

By the time an hour had passed, it was a deal Sarah was glad she had made. She felt peaceful and content strolling beside the lake with Brett. They talked desultorily, and he kept his promise and made no attempt to do more than take her hand. Eventually, he looked at his watch and asked her if she felt like venturing further.

"Because I have no intention of picking up my son before I have to," he informed her.

"Where do you want to go?" asked Sarah.

"Marymere Falls?" he suggested. "We've plenty of time."

As it turned out, Brett's idea of plenty of time meant an exhausting run and stumble on her part and a brisk, long-legged stride on his before they reached the top of the steep path which wound its way up to the falls.

Sarah collapsed in a breathless heap against the railing when they arrived, much too quickly, on a platform overlooking a deep ravine.

"You don't get enough exercise," Brett accused her. "A short walk like that shouldn't wind you."

"Huh. The day I read an article with the title 'How to Use a Rubber Band to Strengthen and Tone your Muscles,' I knew exercise wasn't for me," retorted Sarah, who had learned long ago to defend herself against fitness fiends. Both her mother and Angela suffered occasional bouts of fitness frenzy. "Anyway, I wouldn't *be* winded if you didn't walk like an express train," she added.

"Trains don't walk," replied Brett, stating the obvious.

"No, and neither do you. That wasn't a walk, that was a speed test."

He grinned. "Sorry. I'm used to doing things on the run. It's a habit one gets into around Tony."

"Yes, but I don't live with Tony," snapped Sarah.

"No." He glanced at her sharply, and she wondered why she had a sense that there was something he wanted to say but wasn't going to. "You don't, do you? But now that we're here I'd appreciate it if you'd stop complaining and make an effort to enjoy the view."

"Complaining," she exclaimed. "That's not fair..."

"No, I don't suppose it is. Now shut up and look at the view."

"Well, of all the..." Sarah began. Then she took in the broad grin spreading across his face and knew that she was reacting exactly as he intended. Snapping her mouth shut, she raised her eyebrows haughtily and turned to survey the falls.

At once Brett's goading faded into insignificance beside the splendor of the shimmering silver stream which tumbled down through the trees to break into foaming flakes on the rocks. Beside the falls a carpet of rippling greenery waved gently in the wind of the rushing waters.

It was cool here, peaceful beneath the rain forest's heavy foliage, and, in spite of the noise of the water, small butterflies fluttered in and out of the light. Watching them, Sarah relaxed and turned to smile up at Brett, not caring any more that he had blamed her for being out of breath and then calmly accused her of complaining.

When he put his arm lightly around her waist she didn't even attempt to move away. Then, after a while, his hand dropped down over her hip and began to spread out gently across her jeans.

She gasped, almost paralyzed with shock at the blaze of longing that steamed up through her body—and immediately Brett released her and stepped back.

"Don't worry," he said dryly. "That wasn't a prelude to rape."

"I didn't think it was," she said quickly, not troubling to explain that she had been so stunned by her own reaction to his casual caress that she hadn't paused to think at all.

"Good. Come on, then, we'd better wend our way home. I expect by now the delightful lady who volunteered to cope with Tony as well as her own delinquent is bitterly regretting her kindly impulse."

"I'm sure she isn't," said Sarah, as they started back to the car. "He's a perfectly normal nine-year-old, you know."

"I suppose so," he agreed gloomily, fixing a bleak eye on a pool of sunlight high up among the branches above them. After a while he shot her a quick, considering look that she didn't see, and inquired thoughtfully, "Do you like children, Sarah Malone?"

"Of course," said Sarah.

But there was something in the way he had asked the question that she didn't altogether understand. Something that was almost—what? Speculative? Hopeful? She wasn't sure, but whatever it was, she didn't trust it. "Yes, of course I like children," she repeated firmly. "Most people do, don't they?"

"No," said Brett with feeling. "They don't. Miranda didn't care for them at all."

"Miranda?"

"My wife."

"Oh." Sarah stumbled over a root, caught at Brett's arm to steady herself and, when he tried to help her, moved quickly to the edge of the path.

So her name had been Miranda. It was a pretty name. Not sweet and old-fashioned like Sarah. She glanced up at him, wondering if he meant to say more, and saw that the muscles around his mouth had hardened making his face look carved and cold. Was he angry with her, then? Staring at that granite-hard profile now, she felt a sudden quick stirring of resentment.

Damn it, *she* wasn't the one who had brought up the subject of his wife. All the same, she knew what it was like to suffer because of another's unkindness. If Miranda *had* been unkind..."

"Your wife must have liked Tony," she pointed out, deciding that any sort of reaction on his part would be better than this glowering silence.

His skin darkened, and he replied without looking at her, "She looked after him, kept him clean—or as clean as is possible in his case. But then she was always very careful of her possessions." There was such a depth of bitterness in his voice that Sarah stepped back, appalled.

"Possessions?" she murmured.

He shrugged, eyes white-gold and without expression. "Oh, yes, Tony was definitely one of those. But as to whether she loved him—quite honestly, I never figured that out. She certainly made sure he thought she loved him—I'd have seen to it if she hadn't. And Tony's always been a happy kid, thank goodness. But Miranda had no interest in repeating the—experiment."

"Experiment?"

"Must you parrot everything I say? Yes, experiment. She used to say she wanted the experience of having a baby. Said it was part of being a woman." He kicked savagely at a pebble and sent it spinning off through the trees. "Being a woman! That's a laugh, isn't it?"

"If you say so," said Sarah, rather more tartly than she intended. Brett had obviously been hurt by his marriage, whatever he might have done to deserve it, and she didn't really want to add to his bitterness. On the other hand, this conversation was getting altogether too close to home.

"If I say... Oh, I see." Brett came to an abrupt halt, and when Sarah, who had been running to keep up with him, tried to slow down too, once again she found herself falling. Immediately he grabbed her arm and pulled her upright.

By the time she had recovered herself enough to look at him, he was shaking his head and the expression in his eyes was no longer bleak and bitter, but resigned. "You're as bad as Tony, aren't you?" he murmured. "Didn't anyone ever tell you that feet are for walking on, Sarah? Not for falling off."

"Frequently. At least my mother used to. And didn't anyone ever tell you that legs aren't wheels? You always walk like——"

"An express train? Yes, I know. You've already registered that complaint."

"For all the good it did."

"Mmm. I'm sorry. And I apologize for snapping your head off. I'm afraid bad memories caught up with me for a moment. I won't let it happen again."

"It's all right. Do you want to talk about it?"

"No."

Well, there was nothing equivocal about that, was there? Nor about the harsh set of his jaw.

"Right," she said. "Perhaps we'd better move on, then."

"Perhaps we had." He was still holding her arm, and as they proceeded down the path at what, for Brett, was a very sedate pace, he continued to hold on to it, saying he had no intention of performing emergency first aid in the woods.

"I won't fall again," she assured him. "You can let me go quite safely."

"No."

"Brett, will you please let go of my arm? I can manage."

"All right, you have a choice," he said evenly. "Either you put up with a little friendly support—or I carry you."

Sarah sighed. "You do like getting your own way, don't you?"

"I make a point of it."

She didn't answer, partly because she knew he meant it, and partly because she was afraid that if she argued she really would end up being carried down to the car—and although she didn't want to admit it, even to herself, that prospect was altogether too appealing. The sensations already aroused by his square-tipped fingers were quite enough to be going on with.

They drove back to Caley Cove in a more or less companionable silence. Brett appeared to be concentrating on the road, and Sarah was lost in her own thoughts, wondering why there had been that odd look in his eyes when he'd asked her if she liked children, remembering his touch on her body—and wondering why she felt guiltily glad that his marriage had not been a particularly close one.

Not that that was news to her, of course.

For the second time that day she thought of her mother's rumors, and it occurred to her that, although she was prepared to believe now that Elise was just his friend, that didn't mean that she hadn't been much more than that during the days of his apparently rocky marriage. What was it he had said about Elise supporting him through some very bad times? He was fun to be with, of course, but there was something a little frightening about him sometimes, something guarded and tightly reigned in...

By the time he let her out of the car in front of her house, before going on to pick up Tony, Sarah's face was once more pulled into the icily repressive lines which she reserved for any male who wasn't over seventy, under seventeen, or her father.

Brett took one look at her expression, and muttered something which sounded like, "Oh, Lord, the return of Miss Havisham." Then, brushing his hand over his jaw, he asked mockingly, "Training for the Prune of the Year contest, Sarah? I'm sure you'll win."

She glared at him, speechless.

"Good Lord," he muttered again. "Sarah, what is this? What have I done now?"

She looked up into tawny eyes fixed on her in exasperation mixed with reluctant amusement—and it came to her that up to this moment he hadn't actually done anything worse than give her a pleasant day—and laugh with her, and put his hand where it had no business being—and call her a prune...

She started to smile. "Nothing," she replied, staring at a tattered gum wrapper blowing beside the road. "I'm sorry if I seemed ungrateful. It's really been a delightful day."

"Spoken like an unrepentant prune. Possibly descended from a duchess. Can't you do better than that?"

She looked up quickly. "How—better?"

"Thank me properly." He held out his arms.

Sarah gaped at him. "I—I..."

"Come on. I know you know how to kiss."

"So do you," she said unthinkingly, "but..."

"No buts. Come on, do as you're told. Thank me."

He looked so incredibly male, standing there with his legs apart, head thrown back and his full lips laughing a command and an invitation, that without quite knowing she was doing it Sarah took a half step forward.

"That's right," he encouraged. "Kiss me, Sarah."

He was still laughing, but there was something so demanding in his tone, so compelling, that Sarah felt as if she were being hypnotized against her will. Slowly she moved toward him. And then it wasn't against her will any more as his lips closed over hers and once again she tasted the clean, masculine warmth of his mouth, felt his soft, smoky breath on her cheek—and knew the wonder of a man's arms holding her tenderly, in a caress that, for this one brief moment, she could honestly believe would never hurt her.

Then he held her away from him, said, "There. That wasn't so hard, was it? Thank you for coming with me."

"I—thank you too, Brett. It—it was lovely."

He grinned. "Don't sound so surprised. It's not at all flattering." He glanced at his watch. "And now I must be on my way. It's after six. Good night, my dear. I'll see you soon." He put his hands on her shoulders, spun her around and gave her a little shove toward the gate.

She didn't look back, and a few minutes later she heard him switch on the engine and drive off rather fast down the road.

It seemed only a few minutes later that she found herself in the kitchen doing something quick and easy with eggs, but when she looked at the chrome and white clock on the wall she saw that a whole half hour had passed since Brett had left.

What on earth had she been doing? Dreaming? But she didn't dream. Dreaming had been against her principles for—at least ten years.

Another half hour passed, during which she ate the something with eggs—she had an idea she'd poached them but could scarcely remember—and now the dishes were done and she was sitting in the window once more listening to the crashing of the waves. It was a restful sound, endless and eternal, and if she concentrated on it maybe she wouldn't need to think. Or dream?

A car roared by outside, making her jump, and her efforts at concentration were shattered. Now it wasn't the waves she heard any more, but Brett's deep, laughing voice saying, "Kiss me, Sarah." And she had kissed him, hadn't she? If he had not stopped her, she would have gone on kissing him.

"*Why*, you idiot?" she groaned out loud. "Why?"

Well, that was easy, wasn't it? She found him unbearably attractive. And her hunger for love had been repressed for so long...

Yes, but where would it all end up if she gave in to him, gave him what he wanted—what she wanted too, if she were honest? She thought of Miranda, who had not been happy and who might, if rumors were true, have taken her life. She thought of Elise, who had been Brett's receptionist and was still his friend—and of Mary-Jo Somebody, who was "history." Three women—at least three—whose relationships with Brett had failed.

Oh, sure, he was devastatingly attractive, incredibly sexy—and he could be kind and he made her laugh when he wasn't making her angry. But still, his record wasn't promising. In the days when she had made that terrible mistake with Jason she had been able to plead youth and inexperience. Now, if she allowed herself to become involved with Brett, she would be walking into trouble with her eyes wide open. What was more, she knew what would happen, didn't she? Sarah pushed a tendril of hair from her eyes and stared stonily out at the dusk. Oh, yes, she knew what would happen all right. They would have a flaming, exciting, wonderful affair—and then it would end.

The question, of course, was whether she wanted to risk the emotional upheaval, the inevitable grief, that would follow. In short, was she willing to risk being hurt—badly—for the second time in her life?

She closed her eyes and the sound of the waves rolled over her, leaving her mind strangely numb.

It stayed that way until long after she went to bed and then, as sleep at last began to overtake her, she concluded that it really didn't matter, because when, and if, the time came to make a decision—she would make it. Not before.

"Sarah, what's this I hear? About you and Brett Jackson." Clara Malone's voice rang out clear and shrill the moment she stepped into the house.

Sarah, who hadn't heard her parents drive up over the mechanical roar of her food processor, stood with her hand on the doorknob and gaped at her mother's anxious face.

"Me and—what did you hear, Mother?"

"A more useful question might be, What *didn't* she hear?" George answered for her.

"What do you mean?"

"Well, so far your mother has been informed that you're having a steamy affair with your new neighbor, that you're *not* having a steamy affair with him because you're holding out for marriage, that he's dumped you and taken up with a police sergeant from Seattle——"

"A police sergeant?" said Sarah faintly.

"A female one, I suppose—and, last but by no means least—that you're pregnant."

# CHAPTER EIGHT

"YOU'RE not serious?" Sarah stared incredulously at the worried-looking pair on her doorstep. When she became aware, belatedly, that this was a ridiculous place to be holding such a highly fraught conversation, she waved them on into the hall. "Supper's not quite ready," she murmured inanely.

"Never mind supper. We'll eat later," said Clara, dismissing food with an impatient wave of her hand. "First of all, tell us about Brett."

Sarah nodded and led them into the living room. "What about Brett?" she asked when they were all seated. "Are you asking me to pick one of the above? Whether I'm being loved, jilted, ignored or impregnated? Because if you are——"

"Sarah! Really. That's no way to talk to your mother!" exclaimed George, leaping to his wife's defense.

No, thought Sarah tiredly, of course it isn't, unless *you* happen to be doing the talking, Dad. But aloud she only said quietly, "No. It isn't. I'm sorry. You took me by surprise, that's all, and I didn't quite know what to say."

"We're worried about you, Sarah." Clara's voice, usually so assured, sank to a doubtful murmur.

"Oh, Mother, I don't blame you, if people have been spreading gossip like that. None of it's true, I promise you, but really you shouldn't listen——"

"For once she didn't have a choice," interrupted George. "Molly Bracken came around specially to tell

116

us that Mrs. Mackenzie had been baby-sitting young Tony so that his father can go out with you. Apparently Mrs. Mackenzie told Harry Koniski..."

Sarah closed her eyes and tuned her father out. She didn't have to hear any more. It was true that she had been out with Brett three times since last Sunday. He had asked her and she had said "yes" because, somewhat to her own surprise and in spite of all her soul-searching, it had seemed the natural and reasonable thing to do.

They had been out to dinner, to a movie, and once they had just gone for a drive and talked. Brett hadn't pressured her in any way—except to tell her, forcibly and frequently, that her clothes looked like hell and to change them—nor had he tried to kiss her again, and the hours they had spent together had been relaxed and friendly. Most of the time. Although once or twice she had caught an odd, hard look on his face when she'd pulled her hand from his a little too quickly, or made a point of not sitting too close. In spite of that, she couldn't remember a time when she had looked forward to each new day with such eager anticipation. *But*, she told herself repeatedly, there was no question of its going any further. Maybe the wall she made a point of maintaining between herself and the opposite sex *was* crumbling a little, but that didn't mean it was going to collapse.

Her father's voice droned on relentlessly, and she sighed. Yes, she had enjoyed the past week, but all good things had their price, and now she had the usual crop of Caley Cove rumors to contend with.

She knew exactly what had happened. Mrs. Mackenzie had mentioned in passing that she was baby-sitting Tony, and of course that was all Caley Cove ever needed to start the gossip going around.

George Malone finished chronicling the exact route the stories had taken before catching up with his wife, via the kindly offices of her old friend, Molly Bracken.

"So you see," he concluded, "on this one rare occasion, your mother really was the last to know."

"But is any of it true?" pressed Clara, ignoring her husband's barb.

Sarah made a face. "Well, I'm not having an affair with Brett, I'm not planning to marry him, as far as I know he's not seeing a police sergeant, and no—I am not pregnant."

"Well, thank goodness for that!" exclaimed Clara. "Although I was sure it couldn't be true—not after Jason—but Molly seemed so sure..."

"The only thing that's true is that I *have* been out with Brett," said Sarah. She wasn't particularly anxious to impart even this much information, because past experience had taught her that her mother would immediately read more into it than was there. But there didn't seem any way to avoid it.

At once Clara's face lit up, and Sarah groaned inwardly. "It's not serious, though," she said quickly. "We're just neighbors."

"So is Mrs. Mackenzie, but he doesn't take her out."

"No, I think Mr. Mackenzie might object," replied Sarah, smiling wearily. "Shall we eat? I'm sure supper must be ready by now."

She spent the rest of the evening fending off questions about Brett, and frantically dissuading her mother from rushing next door to inspect her daughter's new friend for herself.

"I expect he's out anyway," she said desperately.

"Who with? The sergeant?"

"Probably," Sarah agreed, giving up.

Inevitably this failed to satisfy Clara, and by the time her parents left their daughter felt more exhausted and limp than she had since the last time she'd had the flu. Lord, if all her Saturdays with her parents were going to be like this from now on, she would have to move to Seattle.

Seattle. The police sergeant.

"Are you really going out with a police sergeant?" she asked Brett, when he and Tony arrived in her kitchen the next morning to tell her they were going back to the Game Farm, along with Tony's friend, Joe.

"Am I *what*?" asked Brett.

"A police sergeant!" exclaimed Tony. "But Dad's a man."

And *how*, thought Sarah, choking into a cup of coffee. "Yes, I'd noticed," she replied, on a strangled gasp. "I meant a lady one, Tony."

Brett curled his hand smoothly around the back of her neck and pulled her closer. "I'm so glad you noticed," he murmured. The soft words held an undercurrent of menace. "Now what the *hell* are you talking about, Sarah?"

Sarah sighed. "The Caley Cove rumor mill," she explained.

"What?" Brett's jaw set in that way it always did when he was angry, and the look he gave her was one of utter scorn and disgust.

"It's not my fault," she protested.

He took a deep breath, and made a visible effort to hold his anger in check. "No. Of course it's not. And no, I am not going out with a sergeant. I make it a point never to go out with more than one woman at a time. Apart from which, uniforms don't do any more for me than those tired tweeds you still insist on wearing."

"Thanks," said Sarah. "Then I don't have anything to worry about, do I?"

He made a sound that reminded Sarah of one of the Game Farm's larger residents. "From a uniformed rival, no. From me, if you keep it up, plenty."

"Keep what up?" asked Tony, who was tired of being ignored.

"The successful impersonation of a potato," replied Brett rudely.

"But Sarah doesn't look like a potato."

"No," agreed his father, running his eyes thoughtfully over her jeans and navy sweater. "Not today, she doesn't."

Sarah ventured a small smile, which caused him to add reflectively, "I think I'm beginning to see the light. If you must know, I *was* stopped by a policewoman that day when I came back from moving Elise. But didn't you say something about Seattle?"

"I did," said Sarah glumly. "Never mind, it does make some sort of sense now, and the Seattle part's not at all surprising. It makes a much better story than your being stopped by Constable Smith from Sequim or Caley Cove."

Brett sighed. "Yes, I suppose it does." He stared at her with an odd sort of concentration, appeared to come to a decision, and said, "Speaking of Sequim, I hope you're coming with us. To the Game Farm."

"Well, I don't know..." she began.

"Course she is," said Tony.

"Yes, but..." muttered Sarah.

In the end, of course, Tony was right. She made various halfhearted protestations about washing clothes and scrubbing floors, to which Brett replied carelessly that all that was commendably domestic of her but very boring, and Tony repeated his assertion that of course she was coming with them but to hurry up.

Sarah, head swirling, eventually gave in to their combined persuasion.

By the time they arrived at the Game Farm, she was already beginning to regret her capitulation. Tony by himself was a restless, energetic handful. With his friend Joe to aid and abet him, even before they were through the gates he was planning mayhem, and Sarah had a feeling that any mischief he had managed not to get into with her would be speedily made up for on this visit. On top of which she suspected that Brett's enthusiasm for her company had been prompted not so much by friendship as by self-interest. In a nutshell, she thought, all he really wanted was help with two overactive, over-inventive, thoroughly impossible youngsters. Not that she could altogether blame him.

Her misgivings proved more than justified. The moment Brett stopped the car at the observation tower above the Farm, Tony was out, up the steps and leaning so far over the edge of the wooden structure that it was only by grabbing his ankles that Brett was able to stop him from tumbling to the ground. A minute afterward Sarah performed a similar office for Joe as he too tried to launch himself into space.

Three hours later, after the pair of them had been dissuaded from joining a group of bears enjoying a meal in the sun, attempting to ride a zebra, and getting out of the car in front of a sign saying "Stay Inside Your Automobile AT ALL TIMES," Brett suggested grimly that they had better leave before they were attacked.

"And not by the inmates, either," he muttered, as they drew up outside McDonald's on the way home. "If I'd been a member of the Farm's long-suffering staff,

I'd have fed the pair of them to the nearest cougar. Come to think of it, I wish I'd thought of it myself."

Sarah laughed, and had a brief vision of Brett standing in the dock in a courtroom looking impressive. "Joe's mother might take a dim view of that," she murmured. "But I expect you'd have got away with it just the same. All the female jurors would acquit you."

"Of infanticide? Don't count on it. Hell, Elise still holds the broken glasses against me. But since you're paying compliments for a change—at least, I think that was a compliment—perhaps this is a good time to mention that I have a reprieve next weekend. Joe's mother is a glutton for punishment and she's offered to have Tony again." His eyes met hers, gleaming and seductive. "I'd like to take you away with me, Sarah. Will you come?"

"Away?" she squawked, knowing she sounded like a chicken beating a panicky retreat from a fox. "I can't go away with you, Brett. I can't."

Brett didn't press the point until they arrived outside her gate some time later, but as he helped her out of the car he said again, "Come with me on Friday, Sarah. By that time I'll be desperate for feminine conversation."

"Just conversation?" she asked, her eyes on the gate, the sky, the trees—anything but his face.

"I hope not," he answered with unmistakable innuendo.

"Then I can't go."

"Sarah——"

At that moment Tony and Joe, who had been told to wait in the car while Brett opened the door for Sarah, decided they'd waited long enough, and began to play the "Wedding March" on the horn.

"Hell," muttered Brett. "Just a minute." He leaned into the car and, watching him, she was reminded of her first mouth-watering view of the bottom half of him. The noise stopped abruptly and then he was back. "Yes, you *can* go away with me," he said peremptorily. "Nothing's going to happen to you that you don't want to happen, I promise, and it's time someone coaxed you out of your shell. Now then, Snow Queen . . ." He rested his hand on the gate and leaned toward her. "I've got a busy week ahead of me. Old friends I've promised to visit, a couple of obligatory meetings and—heaven help me—a father and son baseball tournament with Tony. So I'll leave you to make up your mind, shall I?"

"And if I decide not to go?"

Brett's fingers tapped against his thigh. "I am a patient man, my dear," he growled, thrusting his head forward at an oddly belligerent angle. "But not that patient. And if you want the truth, I'm not sure what I'll do. However, believe me, I'll think of something."

He lifted his hand and for a moment she wasn't sure if he meant to stroke her or strike her, but in the end all he did was drop it heavily onto her shoulder.

"Thanks for your help today," he said more gently. "It saved my sanity." He gave her a twisted smile that curdled her stomach, said, "See you on Friday evening. At seven," and walked quickly away to join the two impatient demons in the car.

Sarah, feeling as if she were on a fast trip downhill on an out of control roller coaster, didn't answer, but ran for the comparative safety of her home.

*His* sanity, she thought hotly, as she pulled overdried clothes out of the dryer. That was all very well for him, but what did he think he was doing to *her* sanity? He talked of coaxing her out of her shell, but there had been nothing coaxing about the way he had practically threatened her when she'd told him she couldn't go away with him. And what was he up to anyway?

Had all his careless, easy friendship been nothing more than an act to gain her confidence so that he could get on with the much more important business of luring her into his bed? After all, he knew she had been lured before and, to be fair, he had admitted quite openly that he wanted her. Only—lately he had been so restrained. He had made no demands, put no pressure on her. So why, now, this sudden demand that she go away with him next weekend? Because no matter what he said, if she did agree to go, he would expect their relationship to change.

Irritably she pulled the remainder of the washing from the dryer and tramped back into the kitchen.

Perhaps, though, it was true that Brett's patience was running out. Perhaps this was his way of delivering an ultimatum. There was no doubt he knew that she wasn't indifferent to him. Could he be trying to shake her into— how had he put it? Making up her mind...?

"Damn you, Brett Jackson," she muttered. Then, realizing she still held a sensible brown blouse in her hands, she twisted it into a ball before flinging it at the counter with a sigh of exasperation.

When Friday morning rolled around she was still throwing clothes about and muttering with exasperation. Not because she was packing to go with Brett, but because throwing things seemed to relieve her feelings and clothes were the least susceptible to damage.

"You look as if you recycled the contents of your rag-bag this morning," remarked Angela when she arrived at the office.

"What?" Sarah glanced down at her skirt. It had an uncharacteristic rip along the seam. Then she saw that her beige blouse was the one she had put aside yesterday because it had a stain on the sleeve. "Oh, dear," she murmured. "Sorry, Angela. I don't know what I was thinking of when I got up."

"Your handsome new neighbor, I expect," said Angela drily. "Don't be sorry. It's about time there was a man in your life."

"But he's not in my—Angela, how do you know about Brett? I never said anything...?"

"You didn't have to. It's written all over you, quite apart from the fact that I have a very reliable line into the Caley Cove information network."

"Oh. What do you mean, it's written all over me?" Sarah tossed her head. "And what's all this nonsense about my needing a man in my life? You sound just like Mother, but at least there's some excuse for her. She's happily married."

"And I wasn't?" Angela laughed. "Well, that's true enough, but that doesn't mean there aren't any men in my life. Sarah, ever since your sexy neighbor appeared on the scene you've gone all soft and dreamy. You smile more often. I've even seen you blush, and it suits you." She eyed Sarah thoughtfully over the top of her pink glasses. "Take my advice this time, won't you? Don't push him away."

"What makes you think I'm going to?" asked Sarah, deciding that there was no point in dissembling with Angela. She knew her too well.

"The fact that not once this week have you given me a starry-eyed description of the therapeutic value of modeling ships—not to mention your unusually disorganized appearance."

"Oh." Sarah stared at the employer who was also her very good friend.

What Angela said was true enough. The only time she had attempted to work on her ship this week, her fingers had been so clumsy that she had given up in despair.

And this morning she hadn't even noticed the clothes she was putting on.

"All right, then," said Angela briskly. "I've said my piece. No more good advice today, I promise. Will you have a look at these letters for me, please?"

Sarah nodded and drifted thoughtfully into her office. Her boss was right, of course. She *had* been behaving like a teenager in love for the last few days. She frowned down at her blotter and tapped it impatiently with her pen. What was she thinking of? In love? She wasn't in love. Brett had awakened some perfectly ordinary physical needs that she hadn't allowed herself to dwell on for many years. That was all. But she had vowed never to fall in love again and she certainly wasn't doing it now. It wasn't worth it. Not when all Brett wanted was an outlet for his own physical hungers.

Right, Sarah, she thought, stabbing the pen viciously into the blotter. So you want Brett, he wants you? What's holding you back?

Common sense, she answered herself. You know what happened last time.

Yes. Last time she had fallen in love. This time she wasn't going to. Only that didn't answer the question of whether she was going away with Brett tonight, did it? The tip of her pen snapped off and flew against the window. Damn. No, it most certainly didn't.

Yes, it did. Of course she wasn't going. The whole idea was absurd. Not worth considering.

She picked up another pen and began, very methodically, to check over Angela's letters.

"Sarah! Open up. I know you're there."

Sarah stared dully at the shuddering door and wondered if its hinges would hold. She was standing with her back against the wall in her front hallway, her gaze riveted on the doorframe which was currently under attack.

"Sarah! I said open up. Or do you want me to break down this door?"

It wouldn't break, she thought. No, surely it wouldn't. Not even Brett in a rage could destroy the handiwork of one of the Peninsula's best builders. Or could he? She thought vaguely of a comment Tony had made about his dad breaking chairs when he was angry. Well, he was certainly angry now. The noise he was making left her in no doubt of that.

"Dammit, Sarah, at least you owe me the courtesy of an answer."

The door shuddered again and creaked ominously. Sarah, feeling like a condemned woman on her way to the scaffold, walked slowly across the narrow hall and put her hand on the bolt.

Brett was right. She did owe him the courtesy of an answer.

Closing her eyes, because she was afraid of what she might see in his, very slowly she opened the door.

He was standing on the top step with one fist raised above his head to strike again. When he did not immediately erupt across the threshold, or attempt to touch her, she opened her eyes—cautiously.

"For Pete's sake, woman, don't look at me as if you expect me to assault you. Although I'd like to." With an exclamation of impatience he put both large hands on her shoulders, pushed her inside and closed the door surprisingly quietly behind him. "Right," he said, his eyes like molten gold on her face. "Now what's this about, Sarah? Do I take it you don't want to come with me?"

She could tell from the way his hands tightened on her arms that he was making a superhuman effort to keep his temper at least partly under control.

"I—no, I think it's better not, Brett."

"Why is it *better*?" His derisive voice snapped like the crack of a whip.

"Because—because I told you, I don't want any involvement, Brett. We can be neighbors, can't we? Friends, as we've been for the past few weeks. If I go away with you for a weekend it will be all different. I'll be..." She hesitated.

"Compromised?" he jeered, finishing the thought for her. "Well, just in case you hadn't noticed, Snow Queen, we are involved. We've been much more than friends for the past few weeks. Also, as far as Caley Cove is concerned, you're probably compromised already."

His fingertips were digging into the fabric of her blouse now, and she winced. Immediately Brett released her and stood with his hands hanging loosely at his sides, looking maddeningly virile and sexy.

"I suppose you're right," said Sarah bitterly. "Caley Cove knows I made a fool of myself once. No doubt they're waiting for me to make the same mistake again."

"So that's what you think loving me would be? Making a fool of yourself. Thanks for the compliment, Sarah."

"Loving you?" she whispered. "But I don't..."

"No, you've made that quite clear. On more than one occasion. I meant loving in a euphemistic sense, naturally." His voice was very hard and cold.

Loving in a euphemistic sense? Oh. She understood now. He had used the word love as a euphemism for—sex. Naturally.

"Brett, I think you'd better go. I'm not going with you and there's no sense in prolonging this scene."

"Isn't there?" His sensuous mouth curved in a peculiar grimace. "Isn't there, Sarah? But don't you remember? I said my patience was wearing very thin, and that if you wouldn't come with me I'd—think of something."

Sarah moistened her lips, unaware that the soft, sensual gesture and the allure of her wide, anxious eyes were inflaming him beyond endurance.

"And what have you thought of?" she asked, putting her hands behind her back and staring up at him defiantly. "You can hardly kidnap me, Brett. It's illegal."

"So it is. Then there's only one alternative, isn't there?"

"Alternative?"

"Yes. This."

As she continued to gaze up at him, every muscle in her body tensed to resist whatever he might do next, he reached for her like a gambler scooping up his winnings, caught her around the hips and dragged her against him. At once she could feel his angry arousal as his hard body stiffened against her soft one, and she let out a small, meaningless cry. In the next instant he had lowered his burnished head and covered her lips with his own fiercely demanding mouth.

She could feel his hands circling her hips, pressing into her flesh in spite of the thick material of her skirt, and even as she started to struggle she found herself weakening. Desire was raging up in her right from the bottoms of her feet, and it was lighting every nerve end in her body, making her tremble, liquefying her veins so that, as his kiss deepened and became more than just an outlet for anger, she knew that, whatever the consequences, for a while at least, Brett's threat to think of something had succeeded.

His tongue moved against her teeth, and with a soft, unconscious sigh she opened her mouth to him fully, wrapped her arms tightly around his neck and savored his warm, sweet, sensuous masculine heat.

"Sarah," he murmured huskily, an endless time later. "Sarah, what am I going to do with you? I know what I want to do, but..."

She twisted her fingers through his thick, glossy hair and smiled dazedly. "I don't know," she whispered. "I just don't know, Brett. Not now. I can't think clearly when you're near me."

"Good," he growled. "When you start to think you always argue with me. But I'm near you now——" he paused to pull her head against his chest "—so don't even think of thinking. Just come with me."

"Where?" asked Sarah, her ear against his rapidly beating chest. "Come where, Brett?"

"Anywhere. To the end of the world, if you like."

She lifted her face and laughed tremulously. "That's a long way. What about Tony? And the animals?"

"Well," he drawled, "the prospect of a vacation from those roving furballs is not without its appeal. Tony, I admit, presents a problem."

"He does, doesn't he? We could go to Port Townsend, though. It's close."

His eyes narrowed. "So close that you could run back home if you got frightened?"

Abruptly she pulled away from him and stood with her palms pressed against the wall. "Perhaps. I don't know. Would you still want me to come? On that basis?"

Brett stared at her big, worried eyes, at her soft body now held rigidly away from him against the wall, and saw the faint trembling of her mouth that she was trying so hard to control. And as Sarah stared back at him, she knew that in some obscure way she had won half the battle.

He swore silently to himself and then said quietly, "Yes, Snow Queen. If that's the choice I have, then—yes, I can live with it."

He held out his hand and Sarah accepted it gingerly.

His eyebrows rose in cynical amusement. "It's all right. I'm not planning to attack you on the spot. I suppose you haven't packed any clothes yet, have you?"

"No, but it won't take long." She hesitated, her hand still loosely in his. "Brett, what are you doing about the animals while we're gone?"

"What's this, a delaying tactic? You'll have to do better than that. Mrs. Mackenzie's looking after them. Go and get packed, Sarah."

He spoke in the sort of voice that expected immediate compliance and, taking a deep breath, she pulled away from him and went to get her small suitcase. As she heaved it out of the closet Brett came up behind her and said autocratically, "And no brown tweed or navy armor."

"I don't have anything else."

"Good grief. Wear your jeans, then, and I'll buy you some decent clothes tomorrow."

"My clothes are decent."

"I know. That's just the trouble."

Sarah glanced up at him and saw that although he was smiling, behind the smile was an implacable determination to have things his own way.

"You are not buying me clothes, Brett Jackson," she informed him tartly.

"Then buy your own."

"I'm perfectly content with what I have."

"Well, I'm not."

"That's your problem. You don't *have* to take me away, you know. Not if you don't want to be seen with me."

"I do want to be seen with you. But not in those hideous clothes."

Sarah glared at him. "If you think I'm so hideous, I really don't see why you bother."

"I don't think you're hideous. I think you're quite beautiful. Which is why you will *stop* dressing like a neat but ancient potato and start to look like a woman."

"Who says?" demanded Sarah, resorting to a favorite retort of her childhood.

"I do." Quite suddenly he stepped forward and seized her around the waist, and at once Sarah felt her resistance crumbling.

Brett felt it too. "You see," he said softly. "I told you you always argue when you think. Now stop thinking and do what you're told for once."

"Which is?"

"Put on those sexy jeans, pack your night things and get a move on."

"And if I don't?"

"For goodness' sake, woman, you try my patience sorely." He shook his head and ran his eyes regretfully over her slender figure as his eyes lingered a shade longer than necessary on her trim brown tweedy bottom. "If only you were seven instead of twenty-seven I'd know exactly what to do," he murmured thoughtfully.

"Well I'm not, so don't even think it."

"All right, I'll postpone the pleasure. Provided you stop arguing with me and get ready. Or do you propose that we should spend the night right here?"

"You're not postponing anything, my friend." Sarah gave him a parting glare and lifting her head loftily she marched into her bedroom and slammed the door.

Overbearing, bossy, utterly impossible man, she thought savagely as she flung a nightgown, toothbrush, two sweaters and a gray blouse into her suitcase. Then she paused abruptly to stare down at three pairs of socks and her bedroom slippers which lay on top of the case. Yes, Brett was all those things, certainly. So why was she still going with him?

Because, she answered herself glumly, he was also irresistibly attractive. And he made her laugh. Sometimes.

Yes, that was all very well. She shoved viciously at the top of her case, which wouldn't close. But surely he *knew* he was attractive, even though he never appeared aware of it. Did he hope—no, *expect* that his persuasive charm would overcome her resistance? That in spite of all her conditions and reservations she would end up tumbling neatly into his bed?

What was more to the point, if that was what he thought—was he, by any chance, right?

She shook her head, not allowing herself to take the thought any further. Quickly she jammed the lid of her case shut, changed into jeans and a sweater and went out to join Brett, who was stretched out on her couch flicking through the pages of the paper.

"I'll just phone my parents to let them know I won't be over tomorrow," she told him. "Then I'll be ready."

"The age of miracles has not passed," he murmured dryly. When Sarah came back after making her phone call he added with lazy approval. "I see you took my advice about the jeans."

"Advice? That wasn't advice, that was an order."

"In which case I'm pleasantly surprised you obeyed me."

"I didn't. I was going to wear them anyway."

"It figures," he responded gloomily. But his eyes were warm and seductive as they moved over her, and suddenly she found she badly wanted to laugh. Then Brett saw her lips quirk and he began to smile as well.

"That was a damned stupid quarrel, wasn't it?" he remarked, as he helped her into the car.

"I suppose so," she agreed doubtfully.

"Believe me, it was. And tomorrow you will let me buy you something attractive to wear."

It was on the tip of her tongue to say that she already had something to wear, thank you, but when she glanced up at his face and saw the soft gleam in his eyes and the way his mouth curled up at the corners she changed her mind.

Tomorrow was another day.

As Brett had prophesied, after stopping to eat on the way, they arrived in Port Townsend very late. But not too late to find rooms in one of the town's many Victorian mansions now doing duty as a hotel as well as a tourist attraction. It overlooked the harbor which Captain George Vancouver had described as "the most lovely country that can be imagined" when he discovered and named it in 1792.

Unfortunately "imagined" was all it could be at this time of night, because by the time they got there the sun had been down for several hours.

Brett cast a thoughtful look at Sarah's pale, strained face as they stood in front of the registration desk, and then he asked if they could have separate rooms. At that she threw him a glance of such overwhelming gratitude that he grimaced, and said that she made him feel like a emperor bestowing the gift of life on a Christian waiting for the lions.

"Don't worry," he said resignedly, as he put her suitcase down outside her door and turned the key. "I promised you nothing would happen that you didn't want to happen. And it won't." He placed her case just inside the door and stepped back into the passage.

Sarah looked at him quickly, relieved and startled. "Thank you," she said softly. "It's been a wonderful evening, Brett. Are you—what are—I mean...?"

"You mean, what am I going to do now? I'm going to my room—number sixteen, which is right next door to yours—and unless you have other plans I propose to read a fascinating book about pigs—in the vain hope that it may keep my mind off the beautiful woman in bed on the other side of my wall.''

''Oh,'' said Sarah, not knowing how to reply. ''I like pigs,'' she added irrelevantly.

Brett raised an eyebrow. ''At least we have that in common.''

''Brett,'' said Sarah desperately, ''I know you—oh, dear. I guess I just don't know how to handle this. Please...''

''Sweetheart, I told you not to worry,'' he said firmly. ''And I meant it. Now, you go and get your beauty sleep and I'll try to keep my thoughts suitably riveted on pigs.''

Sarah smiled guiltily, although she knew she had no real reason for guilt. ''Thank you,'' she said again. ''Good night, Brett. I'll see you tomorrow.''

''Good night, Snow Queen.'' He put one arm non-threateningly around her shoulders, drew her to him and kissed her upturned lips—so lightly that afterward she wondered if his mouth had even touched her.

Snow Queen. He had called her Snow Queen again, she thought as she pulled her sweater over her head. Funny, he often used that name when he meant to taunt her, but this time his voice had been full of resigned affection. He had called her sweetheart too, she remembered—and also said something about pigs.

She let the soft folds of her pale blue nightgown fall silkily over her thighs. What was it Brett had said about keeping his mind off the beautiful woman in bed in the other room? She stared at herself in the tall, carved mirror over the ornate Victorian dressing table. Yes, tonight, without the protective armor of her businesslike clothes, and still basking in the glow of Brett's admiration, perhaps she was almost beautiful. All the same, as she climbed into the big brass bed and hauled the sheets up around her she had a feeling Brett would say her beauty was being wasted.

She thought of him lying next door pretending to read about pigs, and remembered that she had quite neglected to bring a book of her own. She hadn't thought she would need it.

Well, you don't need it, Sarah Malone, she told herself, fluffing up the pillows behind her, missing them altogether and slamming her head on the brass.

"Ouch," she said out loud, and was rewarded by a faint stirring on the other side of the wall. "Idiot," she added, also out loud, so that Brett wouldn't think she was injured.

This is ridiculous, she grumbled, silently now, as she settled herself down in the bed. Quite ridiculous. Does he really think I'm going to be able to sleep?

But he wasn't going to sleep either, was he? He'd as good as said so. She glared at a picture of florid pink flowers in a cumbersome gilt frame on the wall. No, obviously neither of them stood much chance of sleeping. So why were they both not sleeping in separate rooms? They could not sleep together, couldn't they?

No, my girl, you couldn't, she contradicted herself. If you were together there's no denying that sleep would be the last thing on either of your minds.

She pictured Brett's lean body stretched out next door, wondered if his eyes still held that bright, sexy gleam— and felt a *frisson* of unmistakable desire creep up like a flame through her loins.

Damn. She should never have come. But she had come, hadn't she? And Brett was very close, and she wanted to be with him. She wanted to feel his arms around her, feel his tough body hard against her own. She wanted to hold him, to twist her fingers in his red-brown waving hair, to love him...

She wanted to love him.

Oh, no. Oh, no! She sat up in bed and covered her face with her hands as the truth hit her like a blow in the chest.

And the truth, of course, the truth she had been trying so desperately to escape, was that she did love him—and it had started almost from that first moment when he had uncoiled his body from beneath her couch and then hurled himself across the floor after a ferret.

She turned the light on, stared, horrified, at the florid pink flowers, and turned it off again. Now what? What was she going to do? She could lie down, spend a sleepless night dreaming of what she was missing—or she could get up, knock on Brett's door and let things take their natural course.

Yes, and what then?

Then, said a traitorous voice in her head, there will be tomorrow.

And after that?

After that, because she would never allow herself to be taken advantage of or used again—which meant that she would never believe in a man's promises again—there would be many empty months and years ahead.

But she would have had her night to remember.

Very slowly, almost as if she were being drawn toward Brett by some unseen cord, she put her legs over the side of the bed, reached for her robe and made her way out into the hallway.

Then she lifted her hand and rapped her knuckles very lightly against the dark, polished wood of number sixteen.

# CHAPTER NINE

BRETT was at the door almost before Sarah had finished knocking, and when she looked up at his tall, apparently naked figure in the dim light cast by a heavily shaded lamp she gasped, stepped backward and very nearly retreated to her room.

"Don't run away," he said softly, grasping her wrist and pulling her in after him. "You must have come for a reason. Let's talk about it."

She saw then, as he closed the door quietly behind her, that he wasn't naked after all. He had a cream-colored towel wrapped around his waist and above it his body and his hair shone with moisture.

"You've just come out of the shower," she said inanely. "You weren't in bed."

"Should I have been?" His eyes gleamed at her in the dimness. "To be honest, under the circumstances, a cold shower seemed the only possible option."

Tentatively Sarah reached out to touch the tips of her fingers to his chest. It was true. His body was cool and damp. But the moment she touched it she thought she felt warmth flare at the ends of her fingers, and she glanced up quickly and jerked her hand away.

Immediately Brett seized it and pressed it over his heart. "See what you do to me," he whispered, his lips moving, feather-light, across her forehead.

Sarah didn't see, but she certainly felt. His heart was leaping against her palms as if it were determined to break its way out of his rib cage.

"I—I'm sorry," she murmured. "I didn't mean..."

"You have nothing to be sorry for, my dear. Come and sit down, and then you can tell me to what I owe the honor of this visit."

He put an arm around her shoulders and drew her toward the room's only chair, a large, overstuffed piece covered in heavy crimson brocade. It wasn't inviting, but as he lowered himself into it and pulled her onto his knees she was thankful that he hadn't led her to the bed. She might have come here with a particular end in mind, but just at the moment she was suffering from a severe case of very cold feet.

Then, as she felt his arousal through the scanty cream-colored towel, it wasn't cold she felt any longer, but searing heat. A heat that was flaming through her like a crazily erupting volcano. She gasped, and without thinking put her hands around the back of his neck, because she needed something to hold on to.

"What is it, love?" he asked. "Don't be afraid of me."

"I'm not." She buried her face in his shoulder. "I'm afraid of myself."

"I know," he answered, stroking his hand soothingly down her back. "You're afraid you may allow yourself to be hurt again, aren't you? But Sarah, my sweet, nobody goes through life without getting hurt some time. It's a risk that goes with being alive. And anyway, the last thing I want to do is harm you. I want to make love to you—heaven knows I want to make love to you—and I know I could. But I won't do it, Snow Queen. Not unless you come to me of your own free will, because you want it as much as I do, and are able to live with consequences of—loving."

Sarah trembled against his chest, and his arms tightened around her. The consequences of loving? But there wouldn't be any consequences, would there? Brett would have got what he wanted and she would have had her night of love. In the years ahead she would have a precious memory, but without bitterness, because this time there would be no promises made to be broken.

She lifted her head and looked straight into his eyes. "I *have* come to you of my own free will, Brett. I do want it as much as you do."

He made a sound that was a cross between a sigh and a groan. "Are you sure, sweetheart?" he managed to grate out huskily. "Are you quite sure?"

Sarah put her hands on his waist and slid them beneath his towel. "Yes," she said with a certainty that surprised her. "Yes, Brett. I'm sure."

He gave another groan and stood up, holding her hard against his chest. Then he put one arm beneath her knees, the other under her shoulders, and without another word carried her over to the bed and laid her very gently on the covers.

For a moment he stood over her, staring down with a look that was almost reverence on his face. "You're so beautiful, my Sarah," he murmured. "So unbearably beautiful."

She held out her arms, and then he was sitting beside her on the bed, untying her robe and peeling it away from her as if it were a superfluous silken skin. When his eyes fell on the sheer blue nightgown, they widened and he seemed to draw in his breath.

"You don't wear your armor in the bedroom, then?" he whispered, with a choke of tender laughter in his voice.

"No," replied Sarah, because it was all she was capable of replying.

"Because you don't need it in the bedroom, do you?" he said, with dawning understanding. "Up until tonight there hasn't been anyone to hide from."

"No," she agreed, thinking of Jason, and immediately dismissing him from her mind. "No, there hasn't. But I don't want to hide from you, Brett. Not any more."

He smiled, a soft, tender, possessive smile, and slipped the nightgown down from her shoulders. Then he bent his head and touched his lips to all the places that up until this instant had been forbidden.

As he did so, Sarah moved her hands to the towel, and in a moment that too had gone. Vaguely it came to her that his body wasn't cold now, and that the gleaming drops on his skin were caused by a heat that had nothing to do with the temperature in the room.

Very slowly she trailed her fingers up his spine and he shuddered and whispered against her ear, "You're driving me crazy, beautiful Snow Queen. Do it some more."

He was driving her crazy too as his hands and mouth explored her body, not hurrying, not hurting, but moving with infinite care and tenderness to give her pleasure.

When she finally cried out, "Brett, please..." he took her with the same strength and tenderness, so that as the earth exploded around them in a wild, galactic burst of sensation and color she knew a wonder and an escalating joy that she had never believed could happen on this earth.

As it never *had* happened with Jason.

Hours later, as they drifted off to sleep in each other's arms, content and sated at last, she thought with a soft, dreamy drowsiness that she had always known that Brett would be a giver as much as a taker—and he had been.

For tonight at least he had given her love and happiness. He couldn't give her hope, though. No man could. But that wasn't his fault, and she didn't want to think of it now.

With a small, contented sigh she curled against his side and closed her eyes.

The eerie sound of a solitary saxophone wailed through the air as Brett and Sarah stood on what seemed like the roof of the world above Fort Worden. They had driven there after a late and leisurely breakfast because Brett said bracing fresh air was the only thing which might keep his mind off how much he would prefer to stay in bed.

"We could stay where we are, of course," he had mused, pulling her head onto his shoulder and resting his cheek against her hair. "But this is a small hotel, and I suspect they frown on guests who spend the entire day engaged in delightful but dubious activity in the bedrooms."

Sarah had laughed and said that in that case she probably needed air too if she was not to be led into further delicious temptation.

It had been wonderful waking up beside Brett's warm, hard body this morning—just as last night had been wonderful. It was a temporary wonder, of course, she knew that, but she didn't want to think about the future. Besides, the future seemed very far away at that moment, curled up contentedly as she was against Brett's side. She felt at peace, almost as if nothing could hurt her. Not while she lay secure in his sinewed arms—loving him, as she knew she always would.

Now, several hours later, they stood in windy solitude on the concrete banquette where mighty guns had once commanded the ocean. And somewhere in the dark, empty shell of the deserted fort beneath them a saxophonist was playing a mournful air. It seemed to symbolise the abandonment of the dank, lonely building that had once echoed to the tramp of soldiers' feet, and the noise of men going about their business.

Involuntarily Sarah shivered as the future passed a dark shadow over the sun.

"What is it, sweetheart?" asked Brett, his arm tightening around her. "Cold?"

"No. I don't know," she murmured shakily. "It's the music. It's so eerie, so sad."

"I expect whoever it is just came here because it's quiet, and he likes the atmosphere and the echoes. Do you want us to find him? So we can lay your imaginings to rest?"

Sarah shook her head. "No," she said quickly. "I have a feeling he wants to be alone with his memories. We'd be intruding."

Brett glanced at her face and saw something there which made him say firmly, "I expect you're right. And now I think we've both had quite sufficient air for one morning. It's cold up here. So let's get on with buying you that dress."

"But I don't need a dress," protested Sarah, as they pushed their way against the wind to the place where they had left the car.

Brett sighed. "We've been over this before, Sarah, and I thought the matter was settled. Today's the day I buy you at least one moderately attractive dress, so you can shed the brown potato image for good."

"I suppose you'd prefer an artichoke or a beetroot," she muttered crossly.

"No," he replied, his lips twitching. "I'd prefer a tomato."

"Well, I don't care, you're not spending your money on me, Brett, and that's that."

"But I have rather a lot of it, you know. My clinic's doing exceptionally well. And I want to spend it on you."

"No!" exclaimed Sarah. Then, conscious that she was shouting, she swallowed and made an effort to lower her voice. "Brett, I know you mean well, but I'm not a tax deduction and I wouldn't feel right about spending your money."

"Dammit, woman, I don't want a tax deduction," he roared, losing patience as usual. "I want to sit at a table this evening opposite an infuriating, charming, impossibly obstinate woman who will look like the knockout she is instead of like some refugee from the kitchen garden."

"Some refugee from..." Sarah looked up at him disbelievingly, saw the pugnacious angle of his jaw, the explosive light in his eyes and the way his lips were clamped down over his teeth—and suddenly she burst out laughing.

"All right," she gave in, her shoulders shaking. "All right, Brett, you win. You look just like a little boy trying to make an obstinate younger brother return some particularly prized possession. If it means that much to you—you can have your way."

"A little boy..." He glared at her. And then, very gradually, the explosive look faded and after a while he began to laugh too. "I suppose I did look like a stubborn kid," he admitted sheepishly. "It seems old attitudes die hard."

"Obviously they do in your case," she said dryly, before adding after a thoughtful pause, "Brett, did you and your brother fight all the time—or did you always get what you wanted?"

"We fought incessantly—and half the time I got what I wanted. But we're very good friends now that the ownership of trucks, games, books, planes and who has the largest piece of pie are no longer worth going to war for."

Sarah grinned, liking his rueful honesty, and for the remainder of the short drive into town they talked comfortably about Brett's childhood, and his parents and brother who still made their homes in Seattle.

Three hours later they emerged, exhausted, from the last of several charming boutiques. Sarah was clutching a large box, but now neither of them was talking about anything, comfortably or otherwise. Brett was scowling, Sarah was looking warily triumphant, and both of them seemed incapable of speech.

It wasn't until they sat down to eat at a small café on Water Street that Sarah managed to say wearily, "I didn't want to argue with you, Brett, but honestly, that orange spotted number wouldn't have suited me, and although the red was very pretty it made my skin look the color of mud——"

"Yes, I know," he growled. "And the yellow made you look like a canary, and the flowered job like a herbaceous border——"

"But they did. Honestly, Brett, you'll see what I mean when I wear the dress tonight—with jewelry and proper shoes. Really, it's just right—and I do thank you." She hesitated. "You don't really mind, do you? I mean I can always take it back..."

"No." He shook his head and smiled at her resignedly. "No, Snow Queen, if it's really what you want...and at least it isn't brown or navy blue."

Sarah beamed at him and collapsed against the back of her chair. Thank goodness that was over. For the past three hours they had done nothing but tramp from one shop to another arguing about which dress she ought to buy. Brett might have been right that her usual colors did nothing for her, but that was deliberate on her part— and it certainly didn't mean that he had any idea what colors *would* suit her taste and complexion. In fact he had turned out to be one of those men who had no idea about women's clothes beyond liking them revealing and bright. Sarah shuddered. If he'd had his way she would have come out of that first shop with a dress that made her look like a cross between a South Sea Island belle and a confused parrot. But now, thankfully, the deed was done and at last, with luck, she could relax—although she had to admit that the whole episode had made her feel slightly awkward. She wasn't used to accepting presents from men, and there was something very intimate about clothing.

But Brett had been so determined, and she hadn't wanted to spoil this lovely weekend...

Lunch, after their exhausting morning, was a long and unhurried affair, and afterward Brett suggested that it might now be time to go back to their hotel.

"For rest and recuperation," he explained, tawny eyes gleaming.

But, unaccountably, Sarah was overcome with confusion. She desperately wanted to be alone with Brett, but at the same time she was afraid that further intimacy would, in some obscure way, set the seal on any chance she might have of retreating once more into her self-imposed seclusion.

She crumbled the remains of a roll absently onto her plate and stared at the small pile of crumbs. The trouble, of course, was that Brett had *already* invaded her heart. Hadn't he? So why shouldn't they go back to the hotel? The damage, if damage it was, was already done.

She shook her head, recoiling from the frightening implications. "No. No, Brett. I think we ought to see Port Townsend first. I mean, we haven't really had a chance to look around..."

"Good Lord," he groaned, raising his eyes to the ceiling. "I thought we'd seen everything there was to see in the course of this morning."

"Yes, but not all those big old houses," she pointed out quickly.

"Sarah Malone, you have lived in this part of the world all your life. Don't tell me you've never done the obligatory tour of Port Townsend's mansions?"

"Well, um, yes, but—I was very young."

Brett's eyes narrowed as they rested on her anxious face, now inexplicably tinged with faint pink. "All right," he said curtly. "We'll do it your way. And *then* we'll go back to the hotel."

Feeling foolish without quite knowing why, Sarah nodded gratefully, and a short time later they were doing what Brett called the obligatory tour of the town's Victoriana.

"All those heavy, ornate furnishings," she murmured, as he took her arm after the tour was finished and steered her determinedly up the street to the hotel. "Not my style really."

"No," agreed Brett. "Not mine either, but at least those old houses have a little more warmth than that cozy barracks you live in."

They were in the hotel now, and at once Sarah stiffened against his side. In a moment, as he bent down to fit his key in the lock, she drew away from him and muttered something about getting back to her room.

"Nonsense," he said, flinging the door open, putting his hand on the small of her back and propelling her purposefully in front of him. "You're staying right where I can get my hands on you, as I've been aching to do all afternoon. I have plans for us for the next couple of hours, my dear, so you needn't think you're running away." He saw her small nose tilt indignantly, and observed the mutinous slant to her mouth. "Okay," he said, less autocratically. "I'm sorry, Sarah. I didn't mean to insult your home. At least it's clean and neat, which is more than can be said for mine in its current chaos."

"But you think it's cold and unwelcoming," she accused him. "You're just like my mother."

"I am not in the least like your mother, and you can wipe that pout off your face. At once. Because I'm about to prove to you just exactly how unlike her I am."

Sarah opened her mouth to tell him indignantly that she never pouted, but the words were left unsaid because in the next instant he had enfolded her in his arms to close her protesting lips with a kiss. Then he spun her around, gave her a brisk pat on the bottom and told her to get into bed.

"But——" she began automatically.

"No buts," said Brett, coming up behind her and wrapping his arms around her ribs.

She felt the strong length of his body against her back, breathed in his heady male scent and heard him whispering unbelievably erotic suggestions in her ear—and after that there weren't any buts at all as she turned to clasp him urgently around the waist and the two of them sank together onto the bed.

Later, when Brett glanced at the watch he hadn't taken off and said that if they were going to eat at all they'd better get on with it, Sarah smiled impishly at him across the pillow and pointed out that in that case he'd have to let her get up.

"And I am going back to my own room," she said firmly.

"All right," he agreed. "I know you're not one of those maddening women who take two hours to put on one dress and six layers of makeup, so I suppose there's a slight chance I may get to eat before Christmas. Don't be long."

Sarah aimed a playful punch at his stomach and jumped up before he could catch her.

Half an hour later she was back, and when Brett took in the slim figure before him dressed in pale honey-colored silk with a V-shaped neck, softly draped bodice and a skirt which clung in all the right places without in any way impeding her movements, his eyebrows rose appreciatively, and he let out a low, approving whistle.

"You see," said Sarah smugly. "I told you that with deep red sandals and my garnets it would be all right."

"All right?" echoed Brett. "It's more than all right, Sarah—it's an aphrodisiac." He took a businesslike step toward her. "And definitely meant to be taken off."

"Yes, but not now." She laughed, moving quickly away from him. "You look quite alluring yourself, Brett. That charcoal suit makes you seem very—powerful."

"I'll remember that the next time you try to argue with me," he said dryly.

"But I *never* argue with you," she teased, folding her hands in front of her and looking demure.

Brett rolled his eyes up. "Then heaven help me if you ever do," he muttered, taking her arm and guiding her down the hall.

The restaurant he had chosen was quiet and elegant, the heavy tables and chairs and the big, carved oak fireplace in keeping with the atmosphere of the town. Sarah smiled when they were shown to a secluded alcove beneath an intimidating portrait of a severely bearded founding father.

"It's perfect," she chortled. "No one would dare get up to anything with that face glowering down at them. Which is just as well, as we came here to eat, Brett Jackson—and you can stop looking hopefully at my cleavage. I took great care to see that nothing would show that wasn't meant to."

"So I don't see," he replied, so lugubriously that Sarah laughed again.

They both laughed a lot that evening, and it wasn't until the coffee came, after a mouth-watering meal of salad, poached trout with hazelnuts, and French pastries, that the conversation finally turned serious.

Sarah made a casual comment about a petit point picture hanging on the opposite wall, and Brett replied without much interest, "Mmm. Miranda used to produce a lot of those. Our house was infested with them."

"You should have called the exterminator," she grinned. "Didn't you like them?"

"No, I didn't. But they kept her occupied."

So Miranda had needed to be kept occupied, had she? More evidence that Brett's marriage had not been made in heaven. She studied his face discreetly across the table and saw that it had gone all still and withdrawn. The harsh line of his mouth and the slight flaring of his nostrils, not to mention the cold gold of his eyes, brought all her concerns about his past crashing back.

After all, what did she really know about this man— except that she loved him?

"Brett," she said carefully, "perhaps I have no right to ask, and I know you once told me you didn't want to talk about it, but—those rumors about your marriage—are they—are they true?"

For a moment his eyes seemed filled with an unbearable pain, and Sarah wished she hadn't spoken. Then he rested his large hands on the table, leaned back in his chair, and said heavily, "Ah. Of course. I knew as much."

"Knew what?"

"That you'd heard those ugly stories. I was almost sure they'd traveled to Caley Cove."

"*All* rumors travel to Caley Cove," she replied gloomily.

His face had been a mask, carved in bronze, but now the mask cracked, and he smiled, a thin, unamused smile. "So it seems," he said. "And I suppose you believed them—just like all the rest."

Sarah shook her head. "Not really. I didn't *want* to believe them, but I couldn't help wondering..."

"That's what I thought."

She frowned. "So *that's* why you acted like a bad-tempered bear every so often. You actually believed I..." She paused. "But—if you thought that, and if the stories aren't true, why didn't you say something——?"

"Why should I?" his voice rapped out, hard and abrasive. "I had nothing to apologize for. And I'm not in the habit of pandering to gossip."

"Yes," said Sarah, staring down into her cup. "Yes, I see."

And she did see. Of course Brett would consider it a sign of weakness to explain himself—even if, in fact, he *did* have something to apologize for. He would feel that people could either accept him as he was, with no explanations, or be damned to them. She supposed that included her.

He was watching her now with an odd, shadowed look on his face. "I presume," he said grimly, "that when you referred to the rumors about my marriage you really meant rumors about my wife's death."

"Well—yes. But don't they go together?"

He shrugged. "I suppose so. We were reputed to be unhappy together, for reasons which I don't intend to go into, so of course according to the gossips I was finding consolation elsewhere——"

"With Elise?"

"That's right. She was a perfectly satisfactory receptionist, but at that point she felt she had to leave. And *no*," he added harshly, before she could frame the question he saw in her eyes, "I was *not*, at the time, having an affair with her. That happened much later and it didn't last for very long. But when Miranda died, naturally the word went around that it was suicide."

"But it wasn't," said Sarah with sudden conviction. "She didn't take her own life, did she?"

Brett passed a hand wearily over the back of his neck. "Not in the way you mean. It was an accident."

"Do you—do you mind——?"

"Do I mind telling you what happened? I suppose not. You have a right to know, and I'd rather you heard the truth from me than some warped version of the truth from a gossip-mongering harridan with nothing better to do than whisper about her neighbors behind their backs."

There was such bitterness in his voice that, involuntarily, Sarah shivered.

Oh, dear, she thought. Mother's not exactly a harridan, but—oh, dear. Then she saw that Brett was frowning at her, and remembered that it didn't matter about her mother because he had never met her and in all probability never would.

"I—yes, you're right," she said hastily. "At least you know what really happened."

"Oh, yes, I know," he said bleakly, drumming his fingers on the table. "To put it baldly, I came home from delivering a litter of kittens to an overindulged cat who was quite capable of conducting the business on her own—and found Tony asleep in his bed and..." He closed his eyes. "And Miranda dead in her chair. She'd been watching television."

"Oh, how terrible for you. Oh, Brett, I'm so sorry..."

His lips twisted in a sneer and he turned away from her—but not before she'd seen his eyes. They made her want to cry.

"No need to be that sorry," he said brutally, not looking at her. "Yes, it was terrible, but—the fact is, the rumors weren't entirely false. Miranda and I were not happy together. Heaven knows I didn't wish her dead, but—well, it wasn't as if I'd lost the love of my life. Not by that time."

Sarah stared at the fine white lines beside his mouth, heard the grating harshness in his throat. "You mean you were relieved?" she asked, horrified.

"No. I wasn't relieved." He turned back to her, his hand pressed against his forehead, hiding his face. "Believe it or not, I missed her for a long time. It's often better to have someone—even someone you only fight with—than no one at all. It was hard coming home to that empty house. Hard on Tony, too. That's why we moved to the apartment."

"Yes, I see," said Sarah slowly, not sure whether she should mention now that he still hadn't told her why Miranda died. The memory might be more than he could bear.

But he knew she was waiting. "It wasn't suicide," he said, lowering his hand and taking a long, rasping breath. "She wasn't a happy woman—sometimes I wonder if she was ever capable of happiness. Although I tried. Lord knows I tried. When we moved from Seattle to Port Angeles she missed her friends and that made it even worse. Then I found she was trying to escape from her demons by picking up strange men in bars. She told me she'd joined a bridge club, and I was glad for her. Glad that she was getting out at last. Until I found out the truth——"

"But surely——" Sarah swallowed, hurting for him. "Surely then everyone must have known——"

"No. I was the only one who knew. I found out by accident when I had to get a last-minute sitter for Tony so I could attend an emergency a long way out of town. An old friend's dog got hit by a car. I fixed him up, but on the way home my truck broke down. And there was Miranda—with a man. You see, she was pretty cagey too, only going to out of the way places. No one but the two of us ever knew." He picked up his coffee and drained it as if he were downing hemlock.

"Oh, Brett," whispered Sarah. "You must have suffered so much..."

The lines around his mouth deepened. "It wasn't easy." He shrugged. "But I survived." After a pause he added grimly, "Miranda must have suffered, too. I couldn't help her. I wanted to. I tried to. But it was a losing battle, and it wasn't long before her permanent discontent produced headaches, for which she took countless pills. On the night she died, she must have run out of them, and in desperation she took the key to my clinic—it was attached to the house in those days, but kept locked because of Tony—and started rifling through my supply of canine pills. If only I'd had the sense..." His voice trailed off, and he buried his face in his hands. Then after a while he looked up again and went on with what was obviously an effort. "In the end she took nearly half a bottle of tranquilizers intended for the larger breeds. I think she was under the impression that if they were only meant for dogs then she'd need to take more in order for them to have any effect."

"But for pity's sake!" exclaimed Sarah, staring at his grim, set face. "Brett, how could she do anything so—so...?"

"Insane?" He laughed harshly, and the sound sent more shivers up her spine. "I doubt if she would have done under normal circumstances, but according to the inquest she'd been drinking. I suppose when she found she was out of pills she had a few drinks instead. We usually kept a couple of bottles in the house." His voice cracked. "In any case, by the time she invaded my clinic I guess she wasn't in any state to make intelligent judgments. At least that's what the coroner concluded, but nobody wanted to believe him."

"Poor Brett," said Sarah softly, reaching her hand across the table to place it over his tightly clenched knuckles. "And on top of all that you had to put up with people saying those awful things about you. And worrying that Tony might hear them. Did it hurt your practice as well?"

"Luckily even the gossips were very careful what they said in front of Tony, and of course any of my friends who counted knew the truth." He paused, drawing in his breath. "Yes, it did hurt my practice for a while, but people have short memories when it comes to their own convenience—and I was the only vet in that part of town."

"Poor Brett," she said again. "I'm so sorry I brought it all up, but—you can't blame yourself for Miranda's death."

"Can't I?"

"No, of course not. You couldn't have known——"

"That she'd take those pills? No, I couldn't, but if I'd thought of it she'd still be alive."

"But how could you think of it?" cried Sarah, turning away from the anguish in his face. "Oh, Brett, I am so sorry I brought it all back——"

"Don't be." He picked up her hand and the look he gave her held tenderness as well as the memory of past grief. "I'm glad you know. I'm just not in the habit of discussing it, or I would have told you before."

She heard the sincerity in the firm timbre of his voice, and had a sense that in a way he was relieved. Perhaps, at last, Brett had come to terms with the ghost of his unfortunate Miranda. There was a warm light in his eyes now as they moved over her that made her feel all soft inside. Soft, and a little guilty that in all the time she had known Brett she had been so wrapped up in her own problems that she had given very little thought to his. And on the heels of this realization came the reluctant acknowledgment that perhaps her own self-absorption was the reason she'd been alone for ten years—waiting, like Sleeping Beauty, for Brett to come and wake her with a kiss. Now, suddenly, she wanted to make it up to him, to make up for all his past grief, for thinking more of herself than of him, and for bringing up a subject which she knew had caused him pain.

There were still unanswered questions, of course. In the main, Brett seemed to blame Miranda for their failed marriage, and she could see why. But it always took two, didn't it? What had happened to sour what must have started out as the union of two people in love?

Then she saw that he was smiling his twisted smile at her, and for the moment unanswered questions didn't matter. She only wanted to give comfort.

She smiled back, a mischievous, deliberately seductive smile. "Let's go home," she said quietly.

"Home?" he repeated, responding to her mood as she watched him make a conscious effort to push away memories of the past. "That doesn't mean Caley Cove, does it? Because I'm not sure I can wait that long, Snow Queen."

"Neither can I," admitted Sarah.

A few minutes later they were once more standing in the hallway outside Brett's hotel room. But this time Sarah made no sullen suggestion about returning to her own accommodation.

The next morning Brett sat up in bed, gazed down at the woman still sleeping quietly beside him, cupped his hands around her face to waken her gently—and, when she opened her eyes and smiled, said huskily, "I love you, Sarah. Will you marry me? Right away?"

# CHAPTER TEN

SARAH'S eyes, which had been all dewy and soft with sleep, flew open as she gasped and sat up.

"What?" she muttered inanely, pulling the sheet up to her neck. "What did you say, Brett?"

"You heard what I said. I want to marry you."

"No!" Her response was almost a cry of pain.

Brett winced, then his eyes met hers, holding them in a hard look from which she could not turn away. "Don't you love me, Sarah?"

The words were spoken quietly, without emphasis, but she heard the tension, the vulnerability behind them— and she knew that she had no choice but to tell him the truth.

"Yes," she said, and then, reacting to a surprising moisture in his eye, "Yes, Brett. I do love you. I think I've loved you almost from the moment I met you. But I can't marry you."

"Why not?" he demanded, his hand tightening on her wrist. "Why can't you marry me, Sarah. I love you and I want to spend the rest of my life with you." The corner of his lip twisted in a small smile. "You know, in spite of all your efforts to hold me at bay, I've been happier these past few weeks than I've ever been in my life. That's because of you, Snow Queen. Because of your warmth and the laughter you keep trying to repress, and because we share so many things, including, if I'm not mistaken, a love for my impossible son. You've also shown me these last two days that you're a wonderful, passionate, loving woman. Don't throw it all away out of..." He hesitated, staring down at the white mark on her wrist where he was pressing too hard. "Out of habit." He released her abruptly and began to smooth his fingers over the place where he thought he had hurt her.

"Habit?" she croaked. "Brett, I'm not saying no out of habit."

"Aren't you? Then why, Sarah?"

She swallowed, and pulled the sheet more securely around her neck. "Because—because—oh, I know you think you love me, Brett. Perhaps you really do at the moment. But afterward, later, you'll change your mind. You'll get tired of me as Jason did, and then I'll just be a convenience..."

"Damn it, woman, I am not Jason!" roared Brett. "How often must I tell you that?" The lines around his mouth were grooved and deep and the golden eyes were glittering points of light. "Can't you give me credit for knowing my own mind? I will *not* get tired of you, although at the moment I'm very tired of you indeed— and I've never met a less convenient woman in my life."

"Oh," said Sarah in a small, flat voice.

"Oh?" Brett glared at her. "Oh? Is that all you can find to say?"

"No, I—it's just... Brett, thank you for asking me, I don't want to hurt you and yes, I do love Tony. But I can't marry you. I can't marry anyone. I *am* afraid of being let down again, but it's not only that. If you—if you'd been happy with Miranda, if you'd made her happy, I might feel there was some sort of hope. But you couldn't make it work before, Brett, so why should I believe you can now? I'm not big on hope and promises. I haven't been for some time."

"Sarah..." Brett's burnished brown head moved back and forth in frustration. "Sarah, when I married

Miranda I was very young. We got off to a bad start. I can make it work with you—*we* can make it work—because I love you.''

"Didn't you love Miranda too—at first?"

"I thought I did. But I'm older and wiser now and I hope I've learned the difference between love and infatuation." His eyes softened and he lifted his hand to tuck a stray wisp of hair behind her ear. "Sarah, I know you've been hurt. So have I. And I never want you to be hurt again. Can't you trust me? Don't be a Miss Havisham, growing old and faded and bent and bitter, waving your ruined wedding-day like a tattered flag. Take a chance, Sarah. Take a chance on love."

Sarah shook her head frantically, her eyes darting away from him as she sought for some safe object on which to fix them. "I can't, Brett. It's not a matter of love, it's a matter of my own sanity and peace of mind. Yours, too. This weekend has been wonderful but, if we get married, in the end what we've had will turn to ashes. I wanted a memory to hold on to, and I didn't think much beyond that. I should have, and I'm sorry, desperately sorry, if I've hurt you, but in the long run, believe me, please, we'll both be much happier apart." She twisted her fingers together and went on despairingly, "I should never have let this happen, let you get close to me. So—so if you don't mind, I think it will be better if we don't—don't see each other any more after today."

Brett stared at her, his face once more a carved bronze mask. "And that's it?" he bit out. "You won't even let me see you any more? After what we've had together it's 'thanks for a delightful romp between the sheets, Brett, it's been so nice and of course I do love you but that's just an itch that will go away——'"

"Brett," cried Sarah, appalled at the bitterness in his voice. "Brett, please..."

"Please what? Please don't try to wake up the sleeping Ice Maiden? But you've already been woken up, Sarah." His mouth curled unpleasantly and his eyes glittered with a contempt which turned slowly to hostile purpose.

Sarah shrank back before his anger, unable to comprehend that her gentle, loving Brett had turned into this cruel, wounding beast, bent on destroying all the happiness they had shared this weekend. She had been right to turn him down.

But now he was leaning over her, tearing the sheet from her fingers, his hard hands grasping her shoulders, and she could see the sweat gleaming on his tanned skin—and a small pulse pounding in his throat...

"Brett," she whispered desperately.

But if he heard her he gave no sign, and the next instant his mouth was pressed over hers, not gently this time, but savagely, sucking the breath from her body and taking all it could get. There was no giving in this kiss, only a fierce desire to hurt her as he had been hurt. But as his hands moved down her spine, pressing her to him and pushing her back on the pillow, in spite of the pain in her heart she found herself responding to his maleness as she always had. But the moment her bruised mouth softened beneath his, and her hands began to creep around his waist, he lifted his head, rolled away from her and stared blankly up at the ceiling.

Sarah gazed numbly at his frozen profile, saying nothing, and after a while he asked in a harsh, derisive tone, "Well? How do you think you're going to manage the rest of your life without that, Sarah? Don't tell me that in the small hours of the night you aren't going to wake up, wanting me, regretting your decision——"

"I don't need sex, Brett," said Sarah coldly. She understood that he was wounded and hitting back, but she'd had enough. "I've managed very well without it for ten years. Partly, it's true, because Jason never truly touched me in that way, or aroused the hungers that you do. But sex isn't important. It really doesn't matter..."

His reaction to this patently unrealistic statement made her blink, as to her astonishment he leaped out of bed, turned his back on her and began to jerk on the clothes which last night had been discarded carelessly on the floor. When he was completely dressed in the dark suit he had worn the evening before, now slightly rumpled but still impressive, he swung around to face her.

"I see," he said, very clearly and coldly, in a voice that no longer shook with rage, but none the less cut her like steel. "I see. So the Ice Maiden doesn't need sex, which must never be confused with love, any more than she needs affection, companionship or the chance to become a warm, loving woman, instead of a beautiful, cold shell. All right, Sarah, if that's how you feel, get up and I'll take you home. I think we can dispense with breakfast this morning, don't you?"

When she only gaped at him, stunned, he repeated harshly, "I said get up. Let's get this business over with before I'm tempted to do something I might regret."

She didn't ask what that was, but she could tell from the hard look in his eyes that it wouldn't be anything she'd enjoy. Without a word she pushed back the sheets as he lowered himself into the brocade chair and stretched his long legs in front of him. After that she had to endure his eyes following her every movement while she pulled on the honey-colored dress. When she came to the short zipper at the back, it wouldn't move. She struggled with it for a while as Brett watched her, and then he reached across and silently did it for her. She felt the tips of his fingers linger very briefly at the base of her spine, and she shivered. When she turned around he was smiling. It wasn't a nice smile either, one she might respond to, because more than anything it reminded her of a tiger baring its teeth.

They drove back to Caley Cove in a black, unrelenting silence. Brett refused to talk now, and after one futile comment about the rapidly advancing clouds, to which he made no reply, Sarah too relapsed into her thoughts—at the moment mercifully blank.

All she could hear, going around and around in her head, was the mournful echo of a lonely saxophone foreshadowing the end of—what? Hope? Life? Her chance of being happy?

Perhaps, after all, she and Brett could go on as they had been. Perhaps in her fear of further pain she had been too hasty. No. No, that was foolish. She had devoted ten years to warding off pain by keeping herself aloof. And it had worked. She had known contentment. It was only because she had allowed Brett to breach her defenses that she was suffering all this confused unhappiness now. It wasn't habit that had motivated her all those years. It was well-developed, mature common sense.

But when, a short time later, Brett escorted her up the path to her door, she felt as if some brooding, dark-robed messenger of doom was walking beside her, and she couldn't speak. Then, as she scrabbled in her bag for her keys, Brett set down her suitcase and put both his hands on her waist.

"Goodbye, Sarah," he said, his light eyes grimly probing her dark ones. "It was good for a while, wasn't it? I'll try to hold on to that."

There was no trace of anger in his voice now, but when she looked up, startled, she saw that the planes of his face had hardened and aged somehow, and that his gaze was fixed on her with something that was either contempt—or almost unbearable anguish.

Sarah closed her eyes on that look and her bag dropped unnoticed on to the step. "Goodbye, Brett," she whispered, finding her voice at last, but still quite unable to tell him what she felt. "I'm so sorry."

He made a harsh, rasping sound in his throat, moved his arms around her body, kissed her long and hard—and let her go.

After that, without looking back, he walked down the path and out of her life.

A few seconds later she heard his car pull into the garage next door. Then a door slammed. And there was a great silence in Sarah's world which some time later was broken by the soulful cry of a seagull over the ocean and the sound of the first drops of rain pattering on to the roof.

"All right, Malone, this has gone on quite long enough." Angela slammed a stack of books onto Sarah's desk and pushed her pink glasses up her nose.

Sarah stopped typing and looked up warily. "What has?" she asked, without any interest whatever.

"This grim-faced, stiff-upper-lip stuff and the general air of hoping the world will end tomorrow—preferably with a whimper. It's upsetting my clients."

"No, it isn't," said Sarah mildly. "I haven't seen any clients for two weeks."

"Precisely. Because I've been running interference for you and getting to see them first. But I shouldn't have to, and there *are* limits, Malone."

"I'm sorry," said Sarah faintly.

Angela was right. She had been wandering around like a sad-faced ghost since her interlude with Brett had ended so abruptly two weeks ago. At the time, she remembered, she, had assured him they would both be happier apart, but although she couldn't vouch for him, because she hadn't once seen him, she certainly wasn't happier. In fact she couldn't recall ever having felt more hopeless or dejected in her life. Not even in the frightful days after Jason had left her. Now she went to the office, had dinner with her parents, tried to work on her sadly neglected model, picked up book after book in which she couldn't get beyond the first paragraph—and nothing seemed to make any difference. Her life hadn't changed, but she had, and the quiet peace she had known before Brett was as elusive now as snow in July.

Her mother had already clucked and fussed over her normally serene daughter's unusual depression, and now Angela was starting on her too. Only Angela wasn't clucking. She was fixing Sarah with a severely business-like eye and telling her that she'd better stop moping at once and accept Brett's offer of marriage.

"But I can't," protested Sarah.

"And give me one good reason why not."

"Because—because I don't know if he even wants to marry me any more."

"Don't be ridiculous. You're much too intelligent to have fallen for a man who can't make up his mind."

Yes, she thought. Brett had said something like that, hadn't he? Something about giving him credit for knowing his own mind. And indeed she had thought of calling him, many times, because she so desperately wanted to be with him. But if she did, it would all start again...

"I can't marry him, Angela," she said flatly. "It wouldn't work."

"Why wouldn't it? You're both young, you have no money problems, you both like children——"

"Yes, and I miss Tony terribly. But Brett's already tried marriage once and he wasn't happy. Why should he be happy with me? And I *almost* tried it once, and that would have been a disaster."

"Hmm." Angela pursed her lips and studied her friend thoughtfully. "All right," she conceded at last. "Don't marry him, then. But, since male companionship did wonders for your complexion and disposition when you had it, I suggest you either start seeing him again, or find a replacement. One who won't immediately want to marry you but may at least take your mind off Brett Jackson."

"Nobody could do that," said Sarah, with revealing frankness.

Angela shot her a quick, perceptive glance and shook her head. "You're a fool, Sarah Malone," she exclaimed disgustedly. "Never mind, though. If you won't make it up with Brett, I think I'd better arrange a date for you with John Marlowe. He's an old friend of mine and he's taking the breakup of his marriage quite hard, so he certainly won't be interested in anything permanent. At least you'll have that much in common."

Sarah frowned. "Angela, why are you so determined to find me someone else? You never cared about my lack of men friends before. What are you up to?"

Angela laughed shortly. "Opening your eyes, if you must know. Maybe you'll realize what—or whom— you're losing, if you have someone else to compare him with."

"Heavens, is John Marlowe that bad?" asked Sarah, beginning to smile for the first time since she had last seen Brett.

"No, he's very nice, but he's not Brett."

"Mmm. Well, I'm not going out with him."

Angela shrugged. "Have it your own way, but you've got to do something about that face. I can't have my secretary looking like yesterday's meatloaf forever."

This time Sarah laughed outright, and by the time she got home that evening, surprisingly, her mood was much lighter. But it wasn't until a couple of hours later, when she was loading the dishwasher, that it dawned on her that the reason she felt happier was that Angela had forced her to face facts. She *had* been a miserable meat-loaf since losing Brett, a worry and a trial to those who loved her. And it wasn't worth it.

Brett had been right all along. She had turned him down out of habit. The habit of keeping a thin but tough layer of ice between herself and any chance to grow as a woman. Or, as he had once put it, the chance of becoming truly alive. And why should she be the only one capable of a lasting love? Brett had been young when he'd married Miranda. He was older now, confident, secure—and he said he knew what he wanted.

She had behaved like a timorous fool instead of the self-reliant woman she really was.

And in the end it came down to trust, didn't it? After all those years of trusting no man—could she learn to trust Brett?

She was still pondering that question when Tony knocked at her door ten minutes later.

"Hello, Tony," she exclaimed. "How nice to see you."

The small freckled face lit up like a beacon. "I knew you wouldn't mind," he crowed triumphantly. "Dad said you wouldn't want to be bothered, but I think he just meant *he* didn't want to be bothered. He's been an awful grouch lately."

"Has he?" said Sarah faintly, as she ushered him into the kitchen.

"Mmm. He got mad just 'cos Fawcett ate the bottoms off all the towels in the bathroom, and then when Sparky ate the last of the tomatoes off the—the thing that tomatoes grow on, he really blew up. I thought he was going to explode. It was atomic!'' His big blue eyes widened as he mulled over this interesting possibility, and then he added, half regretfully, "He didn't though."

"No," said Sarah, swallowing. "No, I don't suppose he did. But I'm not surprised he's grouchy if the animals keep behaving like that."

"Mmm," Tony replied thoughtfully. "But I don't think it's just the animals. Dad says it won't take long to get them properly trained—or it wouldn't if I'd co—co..."

"Cooperate?" suggested Sarah.

"Yeah, that's it," he cried, delighted. "Cooperate. But he's real grumpy about everything else too. He keeps burning our supper and swearing—he knows some real *atomic* words, Sarah——"

"I'll bet he does," she replied dryly, as Tony's reference to food prompted her to start rummaging through her cupboards. "I'm afraid I haven't been doing much cooking lately either," she apologized. "But I know I have some cookies around somewhere. Would you like one?"

"Yes, please," said Tony, thumping himself down at the table. "Can I have two? Dad burned the macaroni tonight."

"But you can't burn macaroni," she protested.

"Dad can," said Tony, with glum and unarguable conviction.

Sarah discovered the biscuits lurking under the counter beside the soap. She blinked. Brett might be bad-tempered, but *she* must be going around the bend.

"Here you are," she said, offering the tin to Tony. "Although, if you haven't had any supper yet, maybe you should have something more nutritious——"

"I don't like that word," he interrupted. "It always means I'm s'posed to eat something yucky."

Sarah gulped, and began to scrabble hurriedly in the fridge for milk. "All the same," she observed, with her back to him, "you ought to have something besides cookies for supper."

"I did. We scraped the macaroni out of the saucepan and cut off the burnt bits."

"It doesn't sound very nice," she murmured, shuddering.

"No, it was yucky, but I expect it'll be better tomorrow. Aunt Elise is coming over to cook for us, Dad says."

Sarah paused with her hand on the fridge door. "Aunt Elise?" she repeated, in a voice that made Tony glance at her doubtfully. "So—your dad is taking her out again, is he?"

"Don't know," said Tony, through a mouthful of cookie. "Guess not, 'cos he's always home. But he talks to her on the phone a lot. They mostly seem to be fighting, but Dad always fights with ladies and then he——"

"Yes, I know," said Sarah. "Then he kisses them."

"Yeah," agreed Tony disgustedly. "In kitchens usually."

Sarah straightened her shoulders and took a grip on herself. Why shouldn't Brett be seeing Elise again? He had no further commitment to *her*—and apparently Elise could cook. But as a leaden lump swelled in her throat and threatened to choke her she wished desperately that her heart could accept this civilized conclusion without making her feel as if she were being shredded in a thousand pieces.

Then she saw that Tony's eyes were fixed on her anxiously, and she was brought back to a sense of her obligations. "Does your father know you're here?" she asked, with a fatal sense of déjà vu.

"Sort of," said Tony, helping himself to the last cookie. "I said could I come and see you and he said you wouldn't want to see me, and I said you would and he sort of shrugged and kicked the coffee table and smashed his toe—and then he was so busy saying words he won't let me say that I don't think he minded where I went."

No, thought Sarah, closing her eyes. He probably didn't. He knew his son was in safe hands with her, and in the meantime he could deal with his self-inflicted wound. It didn't sound as if Brett was any happier than she was.

But, on the other hand, he had Elise.

The optimism she had felt earlier vanished under a cloud of despair. She had blown her chance with Brett, and even if he was only seeing Elise for practical reasons at the moment—like cooking—it showed that, although he might regret losing Sarah, he wasn't going to let the grass grow under his feet. Surely a man fatally and ir-revocably in love would shun the companionship of other women—especially women they had once been more than close to—for at least a month or two after breaking up with the love of their life? But they had been apart for only two weeks and he hadn't even been able to wait that long before finding what Angela would call a "replacement."

Then she saw that Tony was drumming a foot against his chair and frowning at her.

"Why don't you come and see us any more, Sarah?" he asked bluntly. "I liked it when you used to come."

"So did I," replied Sarah, in a choked voice.

"Oh," said Tony, nodding. "I get it. You and Dad had a fight, only this time he didn't end up——"

"Yes, something like that," said Sarah quickly. "But you and I can still be friends, Tony. I don't think your dad will mind if you come over to see me sometimes."

"Okay," said Tony, startling her as he pushed his chair back and jumped to his feet. "That'll be great." He grinned. "I expect I'll come next time Dad burns the supper. Those cookies were good."

"I'm glad." Sarah smiled wanly. "But now I think maybe you'd better get on home."

"Yeah," he agreed. "I have to let Fawcett out for exercise before his bedtime. He usually plays in the bathroom. That's where he ate the towels."

"I expect it would be," she murmured. "Thanks for coming, Tony. Come again."

"I will," he called, as he set off at a run down the driveway. "See you soon."

She watched until she heard the door open and close next door, then she made her way into the bedroom and lay down on top of the covers fully clothed.

Sarah sat by the window and stared at the thin layer of snow covering the small patch of grass behind her house. In a minute she knew she'd have to make an effort to get dressed, because John Marlowe was coming in half an hour to take her skating.

Almost three months had passed since the weekend when she had gone away with Brett, learned to love him, and lost him, all in the space of two dreamlike, golden days. The memory of those days haunted her now, and she had wondered a thousand times whether she had made the right decision. Sometimes, when she smelled delectable odors wafting from Brett's kitchen and knew that Elise was with him, she was sure her rejection of him was vindicated. But other times, usually in the dead of night when she lay awake gazing into a blackness which seemed to symbolise her life, she thought she was the greatest fool ever born.

She still wasn't sure what Brett's relationship with Elise actually was these days. Tony came over about once a week, and he said that his dad and his Aunt Elise mostly sat in front of the fire and read papers or books on the evenings when she was there. Except that every now and then, according to Tony, she would tell Brett to stop looking like Dracula on the prowl for a victim, and do something intelligent for a change.

"He doesn't really look like Dracula, though," Tony assured her. "He just looks sad."

It was generally on the nights after Tony's visits that Sarah would lie awake—wondering. Wondering if she should throw caution and suspicion and all her memories of past grief to the winds, and go to him. But in the end the conditioning and wariness of ten years was too strong, and she found she couldn't do it. Then she would think of moving away—anywhere—to another town, and she knew that soon, when the time was right, she would do it.

Although Brett didn't seem to mind Tony visiting her, he never came near her himself and, as she hadn't even caught a glimpse of him since October, she suspected he was keeping deliberately out of sight. Her once noisy neighbor had become as elusive as a jungle cat.

That wasn't encouraging either.

No, she thought now, as she left her window reluctantly in order to get ready for John. It wasn't encouraging at all. And those evenings by the fire with Elise sounded depressingly cozy and domestic.

It had been just before Christmas when she had finally given in to Angela's persuasion and agreed to go out with John Marlowe. Her mother had been pushing her too. A few months ago, Sarah would have refused categorically, but she had changed since then, and in the end it had seemed easier to do what they wanted than to continue with her antisocial and admittedly often lonely existence.

"Thank heaven," said Angela, when Sarah capitulated at last. "That face you've been going around with since October has been enough to put us all off Christmas."

So Sarah had gone to a few movies with John, and once they had gone skating at the arena. Then Christmas had come and gone, in a sort of cheerless fog through which she had tried to smile merrily so as not to spoil the season for those around her. The one bright spot, and the one genuine smile, had been caused by Tony's ecstatic reaction to the sinister mechanical robot she'd bought him. For just a few minutes on Christmas Eve, the day had really had some meaning.

She was still thinking about Tony's glowing face as she pulled on a warm brown jacket and looked at her watch. Ten to eleven on a bright, crisp Sunday morning. John wouldn't be long. He was always punctual. In truth she had found his companionship a surprising relief from pressure. They had agreed right at the beginning that it would be easier on both of them to have someone to go out with occasionally—if only to keep well-meaning friends and relatives off their backs. From this conspiratorial start, their relationship had developed into one of casual and totally platonic friendship.

Mother wouldn't be at all pleased if she knew we weren't even remotely serious about each other, thought Sarah, as John's car drew up outside the gate. Angela wouldn't care, though. She just wanted Sarah to enjoy herself so that she wouldn't brood all over the office, so Sarah was doing her best to present a relaxed and sunny front at work.

"Brr," said John half an hour later, as they got out of the car near Caley Cove's unofficial outdoor rink, a large pond on an abandoned farm just outside the town. "Cold, isn't it?"

"Mmm," agreed Sarah, fastening her skates. "Freezing. But it's nice. I like it when there's snow on the ground and the pond's frozen and the sun tries so hard to make us warm. I wonder why it looks so much paler in winter."

"Don't know. Come on, let's get going before this crowd grows any bigger. I've never seen so many people here at once."

It was true. The entire population of Caley Cove seemed to have had but a single thought this morning, and Sarah smiled as a small girl in a red hat cannoned into her and grabbed her around the leg to catch her balance.

When she looked up after they had disentangled themselves, for a moment she couldn't see John. Then she discovered that he was standing at the very edge of the pond staring at a small, blond woman dressed in blue who was staring back at him with equally hypnotic fascination.

"What is it?" asked Sarah, skating up to him.

"Deirdre." Beside her she felt his body begin to shake. "It's Deirdre. My wife. She's come back."

Sarah looked more closely at the young woman and saw that she had gone very pale.

"Go to her," said Sarah urgently. "John, she misses you too. I'm sure of it. *Go on.*"

John gave her a brief, bewildered smile. "She must have known I'd be here," he murmured. "We always used to go skating..."

"Go on," repeated Sarah.

He did as she told him, and a second later a tall man and a small woman in blue were locked in a passionate embrace.

Sarah watched them for a moment and wondered why she felt tears stinging her eyes. Then she whispered, "Good luck, John," under her breath and skated away into the crowd.

Twenty minutes later, after putting on a smiling facade for an endless procession of acquaintances as she dodged her way around the pond, it occurred to her that by now her ride home had probably forgotten all about her, in the euphoria of his reunion with his wife. She hesitated, wondering if anyone she knew was about to leave, and as she glanced across the ice her eye fell on a familiar freckled face.

In the same instant she noticed that just behind the owner of the face was a sign which read, "Thin ice. No Skating Beyond This Point."

"Tony!" she called, waving enthusiastically.

Tony gave her a broad grin and began to skate in her direction. She grinned back and moved at a leisurely glide to meet him. Then, just as he came up to her, his eyes lit with a devilish gleam and suddenly he spun around and skated away from her, yelling over his shoulder, "Bet you can't catch me, Sarah!"

"Bet I can," she shouted after him, speeding across the ice in pursuit.

She was almost upon him when she again caught sight of the warning about thin ice, and realized that he was heading straight past it.

"Tony!" she screamed. "Tony, stop."

But he was too busy enjoying the chase to hear her above the noise of the crowd. He ignored the sign, and as Sarah strained to put on speed she saw thin cracks spreading at his feet. A moment later the ice broke, and Tony's fair head disappeared beneath the freezing water.

By the time he came up again, choking, by some miracle in the same hole, and still very much alive, Sarah was beside him, cracked ice and water surrounding her up to her armpits. But her feet were planted firmly on solid ground, as Tony's were not.

"Oh, you crazy kid!" she cried, as she grabbed him by the shoulders, half laughing, half crying. "You could have drowned, you little idiot." Her heart was thundering against her ribs, but she was so engrossed in towing a surprisingly lightweight Tony to safety that she didn't even feel the icy cold. Nor did she take in, until willing hands helped them to dry ground, that she and Tony were not the only ones in the water.

As she made to lift him into the waiting arms of a big man with a beard, she realized that on his other side Tony was being supported by a pair of strong, masculine arms—which a moment later were lifting *her* out of the water.

She knew those arms. They were the arms which for months she had ached to feel around her again. Only now, as they held her in a powerful embrace, they weren't warm and gentle as she remembered, but ice-cold and dripping with water.

And so was she, she realized belatedly, as she gazed up into Brett's bemused and much-loved face.

## CHAPTER ELEVEN

"BRETT," murmured Sarah, as her wet hands clutched at his shoulders. "Brett, I didn't know you were there."

"Of course I was there," he said roughly. "Who do you think brought Tony out here? I was standing about two feet away from him in the crowd when he dared you to catch him. If you'd moved your eyes a fraction to the right you'd have seen me."

"Oh," said Sarah. "I didn't see——"

"No. If you had you would now be warm and dry instead of shivering like a leaf in my arms."

Sarah, still in a state of shock, thought about that for a moment. Yes, she was indeed shivering, but right now she wasn't sure she cared about being warm and dry. What was more important was that at long last she was back where she belonged.

She turned her face, almost blue with cold, up to his and gave him a beatific smile. "I don't mind," she whispered. "The ice broke, but I feel very warm inside."

He stiffened and stared down at her, his expression a strange mixture of disbelief and hope. Then slowly the harsh angles of his face softened. "Come on," he said quietly. "It's time I took you both home."

Helped by numerous obliging and anxious hands, and wrapped in generously donated dry coats, Sarah and Tony were bundled inside the station wagon.

"Can I drive you somewhere?" the bearded man asked Brett. "You look too damn cold to drive yourself."

"Thanks, I'm all right," replied Brett, grinning at him. "It's not far, and I have some rather private business to attend to."

The man looked from one shivering figure to the other and back again, and smiled knowingly. "Gotcha," he nodded, raising an arm in salute. "Good luck."

"You and Tony are the ones who are going to need the luck," muttered Brett, as he sped off down the track. "I think I'm going to murder the pair of you, or at the very least beat you severely."

"Why?" asked Sarah, wondering why his threats were music to her ears.

"Because you scared the hell out of me, that's why. For a second there I thought I'd lost the only two people in my life who really matter."

Sarah smiled. She knew now why his threats were music.

"We need to talk, Sarah."

They were sitting at Brett's kitchen table drinking hot cocoa. He was wearing an old gray pullover and jeans, she was wrapped in one of his shirts and a blanket. Tony, who had been remarkably quiet since his not very dramatic rescue, had agreed without a murmur when his father had suggested that perhaps he should go to bed until he felt better.

"Do you think he's all right, Brett?" asked Sarah, not willing to talk about anything until she was convinced that her small friend would suffer no lasting ill-effects.

"He's fine. Last seen sleeping peacefully—with Sparky sitting on his feet and Pickles puffing away on his chest. He says they're keeping him warm."

"And you let them?"

"Under the circumstances, yes."

"Mmm," murmured Sarah, wrapping her hands around the cocoa. "So your urge to murder has subsided, has it?"

"In your case, that depends."

"On what?"

"On whether you stop hedging and make some effort to discuss the future."

"What future?"

"Our future, you infuriating woman." He scowled fiercely. "At the moment the prospect of murdering you in cold blood is beginning to hold a very particular charm."

"Oh," said Sarah. She studied his face carefully and saw the dark shadows beneath his eyes, the lines of fatigue that hadn't been there before—and she knew beyond any doubt that he had suffered as much as she had—was still suffering, because although he was trying to mask it with casual banter she could see tension throbbing in every taut muscle of his body.

She stared at him for a long moment without answering his unspoken question, and then she said quietly, "You're right, of course. We do have to talk about our future."

He had been glaring down at the table, but at that he looked up sharply. "Do we have one?"

"Oh, Brett." Her voice broke, and her eyes misted annoyingly. "Oh, Brett. I—I hope so. Because if we haven't, I don't think I can bear it any longer."

She was crying, so she couldn't see his face, but she heard a sound that was a cross between an oath and a bellow of triumph, and the next instant she was on her feet being crushed against his chest in a hug that would have done credit to a grizzly. Then she wasn't thinking about bears any more, but only about her love for this man whose place in her life was, at long last, the only thing on earth that mattered.

Her blanket fell softly to the floor.

"When did you know?" asked Brett, some time later, as he led her into the living-room and knelt down to light the fire.

"When the ice broke," replied Sarah. "I was in the water and Tony was safe, and suddenly it was very cold—and then you were there, lifting me into the warmth—as you've always been there for me, only I was too stubbornly frozen to see it."

"So my Ice Maiden has melted at last," said Brett quietly. "I saw it in your eyes when I held you there beside the pond." He struck a match, and when it caught small flames danced against the walls.

"Yes," said Sarah, sinking down on to the couch and pulling his shirt about her knees. "Oh, Brett, I've been such a fool."

"That, my darling Snow Queen, is hardly news." He hung up the poker, crossed the room and lowered himself down beside her. "Tell me, if you've been as miserable as I have—and I think you have—why didn't you come to me before?"

"I almost did once, lots of times really, but Tony said you were seeing Elise, and you were so cruel and cold that last morning when I said I wouldn't marry you—I didn't think you wanted me any more. You see—it wouldn't have been the first time a man said he wanted to marry me when he didn't——"

Brett swore, so savagely that Sarah flinched.

"But you asked," she protested, edging away from him.

"I know I did. Now listen, Sarah——" He caught her elbows and pulled her round to face him. "For the last time, Elise is just a friend who is kind enough to worry about me sometimes—when she isn't mad at me. And she understood what I was going through because she recently lost the man she loved herself. My other friends are all happily and heavily married, and very little help at all. If you must know, Elise has been telling me for the past three months to swallow my pride and try to make you see reason. We've had some dandy fights about that one."

"Ah," said Sarah. "So that's what Tony meant——"

"Don't interrupt. I haven't finished. We are about to discuss the little matter of Jason, and I promise you, sweetheart, that if you ever compare me to that bastard again you may not live long enough to regret it. Got that? I am not, and never have been, Jason."

Sarah, glancing at his face, so stern and yet so loving, thought how very true that was. She smiled shakily. "I've got it," she assured him.

"Good. And that brings me to your third point." His features, which had expressed so many conflicting emotions, now turned curiously blank as, to her surprise, he released her and turned to stare into the fire.

"What point?" she asked, puzzled.

"The one about my behavior that last day. I was very—what did you call me? Cruel and cold? I knew your sense of self-worth, your confidence in life, had been bruised very badly by Jason. I should have been gentle with you, given you time, instead of trying to hurt you back. Can you forgive me?"

Sarah smiled into tawny eyes which were fixed on her with such tenderness that they almost broke her heart. "Of course," she said softly. "Provided you'll forgive me for being so incredibly blind."

"There's nothing to forgive," he replied gruffly. "At least you tried to be kind. Whereas I acted like an insensitive bastard intent on destroying all the progress I'd seen you make in your struggle to break out of your shell. I deserve to be drawn and quartered. But you see..."

He hesitated, and Sarah knew that whatever was coming was not going to be easy for him to say.

"You see, although you couldn't have known it, you touched a very raw nerve that morning. I was devastated when you wouldn't marry me and I said a lot of hurtful things. I know that. But when I kissed you, and you told me you didn't need sex——"

"It wasn't true," said Sarah quickly.

"Of course it wasn't. But Miranda used to say that too, and in her case it was perfectly true. Her forays into the bars were just a desperate search for excitement. An excitement that, however much I tried, I couldn't give her." His lips twisted and his voice was as bleak as it had been when he said goodbye. "That's why my stupid male pride made me turn on you. And why wild horses wouldn't have made me ask you again."

Sarah frowned. "I don't understand."

"No, why should you? You're not like that, thank goodness, although you've tried to pretend you are."

"But why would Miranda marry you, if——?"

"She didn't have a choice. She was very young and very pregnant and her parents wouldn't hear of anything else."

"But Brett," Sarah's eyes widened, and she touched a tentative hand to his shoulder, "didn't you want to get married?"

"As a matter of fact, I did. I was in love with her. Had been since I met her in Grade Ten. Funny, we only made love that once before we were married. But of course that's all it takes, isn't it?" He laughed shortly. "And she discovered she didn't think much of it. Not unusual the first time, I know, and I was certainly no expert. But she became pregnant, and after that she was never really willing to give it a chance. She resented the whole idea——"

"You mean you never..."

His elbows were resting on his knees and now he dropped his head on to his hands. "Oh, we did at first," he muttered. "After Tony was born. And she hated it. Then after a while she just plain refused to have anything to do with me. I suppose sooner or later we would have got a divorce. Although I doubt if she'd have been happier with anyone else—because, ultimately, I don't think she was capable of love. That was both our misfortune. Anyway there was Tony—and it never got that far." He pushed his hands through his hair, still not looking at her. "Once, toward the end, I got very drunk. That's when I broke the chair and started throwing cups around the kitchen."

"And Tony caught you."

"Mmm. He thought it was a great game. Miranda didn't."

"I can imagine. Brett?" He lifted his head to look at her then, and she asked quietly, "Why didn't you tell me? I'd have understood then why you got so angry every time I played the Ice Maiden."

He shook his head. "I couldn't. You were having enough trouble mishandling your own problems. You couldn't have coped with mine as well."

"No, I suppose not." She stared pensively into her cup, and then said dreamily, "Just think, if we hadn't both gone skating today, we might never have known——"

"Oh, I think we would. Eventually. To tell you the honest truth, my love, I had an idea you might be out at the pond today. I've met John Marlowe. I knew he was a fanatic about skating—and I also knew you were seeing him——"

"Oh, but it wasn't serious," she protested.

"I know that." He grinned sheepishly, the bleak look fading. "But our meeting wasn't entirely accidental."

"Well, of all the manipulating..." Sarah stopped abruptly, remembering that at the back of her mind she had been quite well aware that Tony was a fanatic about skating as well. She cleared her throat and looked up quickly, her expression now pure mischief. "Tell me," she asked softly, "if I 'just plain refused,' would you start breaking my chairs and cups too?"

Brett stopped looking sheepish, and the tenseness in his shoulders eased. "Very probably," he replied, grinning crookedly. "I don't like your chairs. We'll have to do something about our mutually incompatible furniture once we get married. But," he added, eyes gleaming wickedly, "you won't be refusing me, sweetheart. I'll see to that."

Sarah smiled, a slow, soft, very seductive smile that made Brett's heart turn over. He waited until he was finally able to breathe again, then lifted her in his arms, tipped her firmly back on to the couch and, just as he had promised—he saw to it.

Four days later Sarah, dressed in a jaunty red suit with black trim, arrived home from work humming a little tune.

She and Brett, not wanting to waste any more time, had set the date for their wedding, to take place at the end of the month. Immediately afterward they planned to leave for Paris. Sarah's dream of travel was about to come true at last.

George Malone had been pleased, Clara Malone ecstatic—and her approval of Brett as a son-in-law was assured when he informed her that, as Sarah was moving in to his larger house, her colorless furniture was being sold.

"That man has taste," Clara had announced emphatically.

Sarah wasn't sure that Brett's faded pull-out couch and oddly assorted chairs had much claim to anything that could seriously resemble taste, but she didn't argue.

Angela too had been delighted at the news of the wedding. Delighted and thoroughly smug, in Sarah's opinion. "I told you so" was written all over her face.

But it was Tony's reaction she was thinking of now as she pushed open the front door and made her way into the kitchen, still humming. He had suffered no ill effects whatever from his untimely dunking, and when he had come downstairs some hours later to discover his father and Sarah cooking supper he had taken one look at their faces and said knowingly, "You've been kissing her again, Dad, haven't you?"

Brett, grinning, admitted that he had, and Tony said that was good, but he did wish his dad would hurry up and marry Sarah because she cooked much better than Aunt Elise, hardly ever used words like "nutrishus" and even liked Fawcett and the dogs.

If that's all it takes to be an acceptable stepmother, I'll be lucky, Sarah was thinking wryly, as she dumped her bag on the counter and plugged in the kettle for tea. Then, just as it came to the boil, she heard something which sounded like a sneeze. It was a surprisingly gentle sneeze and it came from inside the cupboard under her sink.

She crossed the floor and, very cautiously, bent down to open the door.

A pink nose wriggled at her from underneath a pile of clean dishrags. Behind it, two myopic pink eyes peered doubtfully.

"Fawcett," said Sarah. "Oh, no, not again." She reached out to scoop him up and the little animal snuggled comfortably into her arms.

It was only then that she became aware of another unauthorized noise, a much louder one this time, that sounded very much like a man's voice swearing, and it seemed to be coming from her living room. Frowning, she walked over to the door—and stopped dead.

She blinked, closed her eyes, and then opened them again quickly. Nothing had changed. Two large feet, in hiking boots that for once were not muddy, were sticking out from under her couch almost as if they belonged there. Brown woollen socks covered solid ankles and long legs extended up to firm, corduroy-clad thighs...

"I don't believe it," muttered Sarah. And then, raising her voice, "Brett, I know they say history has a habit of repeating itself, but isn't this where I came in?"

"You left your door open." An accusing growl drifted up from the floor. "And that hairy little Houdini has done it again."

"I know, and although I'm not complaining about the view, darling—you look very seductive that way up— but there really isn't any need for you to commune with the dust any more. I've got Fawcett."

"The hell you have."

Brett eased himself backward and a moment later his body was uncoiling rapidly in front of her eyes.

"You don't look bad that way up either," she remarked, surveying his lean length approvingly.

Brett shook his head. "You're cruising for it, aren't you?" he muttered. "First you leave your door open, when I specifically told you not to, then you kidnap Tony's ferret, then you cast aspersions on a particularly personal part of me——"

"I wasn't casting aspersions," said Sarah, laughing up at him. "I'm particularly partial to that personal part of you. And I didn't kidnap Fawcett, either. I found him under the sink. Did Tony let him out again?"

Brett developed a sudden interest in one of the ships on the wall.

"Aha," said Sarah. "*You* let him out, didn't you? And you have the nerve to accuse me——"

He laughed and caught her around the waist, ferret and all. "Guilty," he admitted. "Tony's at Joe's and Fawcett looked so disapproving that I thought he needed cheering up—I'd forgotten that pink eyes always look disapproving—then the dogs got into the garbage..."

"And Fawcett seized the opportunity to bolt. No wonder Tony's such a terror, Brett. You're as bad as he is."

"Not really," said Brett, planting a kiss on her nose. "But as a matter of fact he's much better than I am at keeping an eye on *you*."

She frowned. "And just what do you mean by that?"

Brett pulled her closer and rested his chin on her hair. "All those months when you didn't speak to me, I relied on Tony to keep me posted. Without his excellent reporting I'd have gone crazy wondering what you were up to. But he told me you were still wearing those atrocious brown suits, so I figured you weren't up to much. If he'd said anything about a little number like this one, though..." he ran his hand down the back of her red costume "...I think I'd have come charging over here to challenge the new boyfriend—who obviously wouldn't have been good old John Marlowe."

"If I'd known that, I'd have bought it long ago," laughed Sarah.

"Would you? We have been a couple of fools, haven't we, Snow Queen?"

"Mmm." Sarah rubbed her head against his shoulder. "Oh, Brett, I do love you. How could I ever have thought of living without you?"

"I don't know," he replied, stroking the back of her hair. "But if you ever think of it again, I'll——"

"What will you do?" Sarah smiled up at him impishly.

His eyes softened as he looked down into her laughing face, and he answered huskily, "I'll kiss you. Like this."

"Like *what*?" yelped Sarah, as something white and furry tickled her nose.

Brett sighed. "Like this," he replied, lifting Fawcett firmly on to his shoulder.

And he proceeded to show her exactly what he meant.

# *Harlequin Presents*®

## is

- ☑ exotic
- ☑ dramatic
- ☑ sensual
- ☑ exciting
- ☑ contemporary
- ☑ a fast, involving read
- ☑ terrific!!

***Harlequin Presents—
passionate romances
around the world!***

# HARLEQUIN

## *Romance*®

### Harlequin's Ruth Jean Dale brings you THE TAGGARTS OF TEXAS!

Those Taggart men—strong, sexy and hard to resist . . .

There's Jesse James Taggart in **FIREWORKS!**
Harlequin Romance #3205 (July 1992)

And Trey Smith—he's **THE RED-BLOODED YANKEE!**
Harlequin Temptation #413 (October 1992)

Then there's Daniel Boone Taggart in **SHOWDOWN!**
Harlequin Romance #3242 (January 1993)

And finally the Taggarts who started it all—in **LEGEND!**
Harlequin Historical #168 (April 1993)

### Read all the Taggart romances!
### Meet all the Taggart men!

Available wherever Harlequin books are sold.     DALE-R

# JAYNE ANN KRENTZ

A two-part epic tale from one of today's most popular romance novelists!

## Dreams
### Parts One & Two

*The warrior died at her feet, his blood running out of the cave entrance and mingling with the waterfall. With his last breath he cursed the woman— told her that her spirit would remain chained in the cave forever until a child was created and born there....*

So goes the ancient legend of the Chained Lady and the curse that bound her throughout the ages—until destiny brought Diana Prentice and Colby Savager together under the influence of forces beyond their understanding. Suddenly they were both haunted by dreams that linked past and present, while their waking hours were filled with danger. Only when Colby, Diana's modern-day warrior, learned to love, could those dark forces be vanquished. Only then could Diana set the Chained Lady free....

**Available in September
wherever Harlequin books are sold.**

JK92

---

### "GET AWAY FROM IT ALL" SWEEPSTAKES

# HERE'S HOW THE SWEEPSTAKES WORKS

#### NO PURCHASE NECESSARY

To enter each drawing, complete the appropriate Official Entry Form or a 3" by 5" index card by hand-printing your name, address and phone number and the trip destination that the entry is being submitted for (i.e., Caneel Bay, Canyon Ranch or London and the English Countryside) and mailing it to: Get Away From It All Sweepstakes, P.O. Box 1397, Buffalo, New York 14269-1397.

No responsibility is assumed for lost, late or misdirected mail. Entries must be sent separately with first class postage affixed, and be received by: 4/15/92 for the Caneel Bay Vacation Drawing, 5/15/92 for the Canyon Ranch Vacation Drawing and 6/15/92 for the London and the English Countryside Vacation Drawing. Sweepstakes is open to residents of the U.S. (except Puerto Rico) and Canada, 21 years of age or older as of 5/31/92.

For complete rules send a self-addressed, stamped (WA residents need not affix return postage) envelope to: Get Away From It All Sweepstakes, P.O. Box 4892, Blair, NE 68009.

© 1992 HARLEQUIN ENTERPRISES LTD.                                    SWP-RLS

## "GET AWAY FROM IT ALL"

## Brand-new Subscribers-Only Sweepstakes

# OFFICIAL ENTRY FORM

This entry must be received by: June 15, 1992
This month's winner will be notified by: June 30, 1992
Trip must be taken between: July 31, 1992—July 31, 1993

**YES,** I want to win the vacation for two to England. I understand the prize includes round-trip airfare and the two additional prizes revealed in the BONUS PRIZES insert.

Name _____

Address _____

City _____

State/Prov._____ Zip/Postal Code_____

Daytime phone number _____
                                        (Area Code)

Return entries with invoice in envelope provided. Each book in this shipment has two entry coupons — and the more coupons you enter, the better your chances of winning!
© 1992 HARLEQUIN ENTERPRISES LTD.                    3M-CPN

---

## "GET AWAY FROM IT ALL"

## Brand-new Subscribers-Only Sweepstakes

# OFFICIAL ENTRY FORM

This entry must be received by: June 15, 1992
This month's winner will be notified by: June 30, 1992
Trip must be taken between: July 31, 1992—July 31, 1993

**YES,** I want to win the vacation for two to England. I understand the prize includes round-trip airfare and the two additional prizes revealed in the BONUS PRIZES insert.

Name _____

Address _____

City _____

State/Prov._____ Zip/Postal Code_____

Daytime phone number _____
                                        (Area Code)

Return entries with invoice in envelope provided. Each book in this shipment has two entry coupons — and the more coupons you enter, the better your chances of winning!
© 1992 HARLEQUIN ENTERPRISES LTD.                    3M-CPN